LOST IN THE IVY

A novel by
Randy Richardson

PublishAmerica
Baltimore

i

ISBN: 1-4137-7750-3
PUBLISHED BY PUBLISHAMERICA, LLLP
www.publishamerica.com
Baltimore

Printed in the United States of America

This book is dedicated to my grandmother, Mrs. Marcella "Marc" Watson, and to my son, Tyler, who were born eighty-five years apart. Grandma, keep ringing those bells until everyone hears them.

Acknowledgements

This book could not have been written if I didn't believe in myself, and I couldn't believe in myself if I didn't have friends and family who believed in me. The people named below are by no means the only ones who played roles in making this book possible, but they played the leading roles and deserve to have their names up in lights.

Thanks to Steven Michel and Patrick Nagle, not only for their insightful readings and suggestions, but for their friendship and encouragement as well.

Thanks to Cindy Anderson for her cover art, Akiko Ikenoue for her cover photo and Chad Husar for his author photo.

Thanks also to Len Richardson, my father, who taught me to write from the heart.

Special thanks to Roberta Richardson, my mother and my editor, who tirelessly cut through the dense verbiage, leaving a clear path others could follow.

And boundless thanks to Mitsuko, my wife, for her patience and love.

Introduction

This book is set primarily in Wrigleyville, the neighborhood that has sprouted around Wrigley Field, home of the Chicago Cubs baseball team. If you visit Wrigleyville today, you will find that it bears little resemblance to the neighborhood I have portayed. This is because Wrigleyville has changed considerably since I lived there.

Of course the neighborhood's main landmark, Wrigley Field, at Clark and Addison streets, is still there and hasn't changed much since it was built in 1914–despite the Tribune Company's best attempts to *modernize* it. The hand-operated scoreboard that went up in 1937 is still there, as is the ivy that was planted on the brick outfield wall that same year. Legendary baseball owner and promoter extrordinaire Bill Veeck gets the credit for both the scoreboard and the ivy.

When I moved into Wrigleyville almost ten years ago, in the waning days of the summer of 1995, it was not the Midwest version of Mardi Gras that it has become today when the Cubs are playing ball. I recall walking up to the ticket booth at Wrigley Field for the last homestand, buying a ticket and walking right into the stadium. Today that would never happen without the assistance of those kind folks who sell tickets on the streets at three or four times the face-value to suckers like me.

As the popularity of the Cubs and Wrigley Field has grown, so has the neighborhood. Half-million dollar condos have replaced the $500-a-month studio apartments where I once lived. Hip restaurant and bar chains now litter the landscape. Much of the charm of the Wrigleyville I knew--and describe in this book–has sadly vanished.

The Ginger Man tavern I wrote about is still there, but it is not the same place that I knew. Although it remains a cozy escape from the predictable sports bars in Wrigleyville, you'd be hard-pressed to find live classical music there anymore, as I have described in this book. The drunken post-game revelers who once were discouraged from entering the premises now seem to be welcomed. That, I suppose, is the power of economics. Perhaps what is missing most, though, is Bobby Scarpelli. "Chicago's best known rock 'n' roll bouncer," in the words of *Chicago Sun-Times* reporter Dave Hoekstra, Scarpelli symbolized the old Wrigleyville. His bulldog-like presence masked a warm heart. Scarpelli died in May 1998, at age 50, of complications from liver disease. To me, a huge part of the Ginger Man and the Wrigleyville I knew died with him.

A few final words about the title of this book ...

A quirk of Wrigley Field is that about once or twice a year, a baseball gets stuck or lost in the ivy. In such a case, the outfielder is supposed to throw up his arms as a signal to the umpire that the baseball can't be recovered. If the umpire accepts the outfielder's position, it becomes an automatic ground-rule double.

Almost seven years it took Charley Hubbs to roll out from the ivy. Being lost with him was an adventure like none I've ever taken. I hope that you, the reader, find that it was worth the wait.

Prologue
A fine mess

Judge Forrest T. Foxtower stood, naked and alone, in front of a full-length mirror. Behind the locked doors of his chambers, he studied the body he'd sculpted. His guiding authority was an article in *Muscles* magazine titled "How to be an Adonis in six weeks."

Like a jeweler assessing the quality of a diamond, he turned, first to his left side, then to his right, flexing his biceps at each turn. Then he turned to face the mirror head on.

With his hands wrapped around his waist, he spread his legs apart and admired the magnificence of his manliness. A twinkle came to his eyes. At forty-five, he once again had the body of the middle linebacker he once was at Lakeview Academy High School.

He could have let out a roar at that moment, but instead he dressed himself, making sure that every minute detail was right, from the Joseph Abboud white dress shirt and the red silk Armani tie, down to the matching gold Cartier wristwatch and cufflinks.

Donning his black robe, he stood before the mirror again, adjusted the tie and combed his Just for Men "Natural Darkest Brown"-dyed mustache with the tip of his left index finger.

Satisfied, he sat down in his padded, mahogany brown leather chair at his cherry wood desk, withdrew a key from beneath his Tiffany lamp, and inserted it into the bottom drawer of the desk. After opening the drawer and eying the files inside, he put the index finger of his right hand on the divider marked "N" and flipped past two files before stopping at a file marked NEWS CLIPPINGS. He pulled out the file and sifted through several clippings until he found the one he was looking for, from the *Northside Beat*, dated October 16, 1993, with the byline of Charley Hubbs, and the headline JUDGE FREES ACCUSED RAPIST ON I-BOND.

A single story, but it had sealed Charley's fate. Foxtower had gone from being the Democratic party's darling, the presumptive nominee for the 3rd House congressional district–an almost certain ticket to the Hill, given Chicago's party politics–to being a political pariah, resigned to a life in which he'd never escape the dark, dirty halls of the Cook County Criminal Courthouse, where he'd languished far too long.

So it was with a bitter taste in his mouth that he withdrew from the desk his diary and silver Cross pen, inscribed with his initials and DePaul Law Class of 1973. He clutched the pen with a strangling force, until it snapped in his hand. For a moment he gaped at the remnants of what had been his favorite pen. Then he let them roll out of his hand, withdrew another pen from his desk, and scrawled into the diary, *Revenge is sweet.*

A sly, wicked smile crossed his dark, chiseled face as he closed the diary, which, along with the news clippings, he returned to the bottom drawer of his desk. After he locked the drawer, he sat there stroking his mustache for a few seconds. This was the day he'd dreamed would come. The smile faded as he pushed the intercom on his phone for Gladys Bishop, his faithful court clerk.

"Gladys, is the name Charley Hubbs on this morning's bond court call?"

"Yes, that's quite a shocker, isn't it, Judge?" she asked in her shrill voice.

That sadistic smile returned. "Yes, it sure is." A cool air seemed to blow into the chambers. "Can you make sure that he's the first to be called? There'll be a lot of people here for that, so I'd like to clear it first thing."

"Of course, Judge. Will you be taking this one?"

Her obedience came with a price. As loyal and trustworthy as she'd been to him, she could still manage to annoy the hell out of him with nosy questions about things that were none of her business–like this one. He knew why she wanted to know and it had nothing to do with the administration of the courtroom. She just wanted to be in on the scoop, the juicy gossip, which she would pass on to every other clerk in the building. The clerks would pass it on to the judges, who would pass it on to the attorneys. From there, it would reach the reporters, each of whom would soon be calling him, asking him questions he didn't care to answer. This vicious cycle he'd seen played out far too often. But he also knew how to handle her.

"You'll find out in the courtroom, just like everybody else." He pressed the intercom OFF button. As he did this, he gazed across his desk at the bronze statue of Lady Justice, standing there so majestically in her robe, a blindfold over her eyes, holding in her left hand those balanced scales.

The sight of that statue, at that moment, raised in him a devilish feeling. Reaching across the length of his desk, he tapped one of the scales with the index finger of his right hand. His eyes followed the movement of the scales as they rocked up and down, up and down, and eventually came to a stop right where they'd started, in balance again. *So naïve. So naïve.*

With an index finger resting on his chin, Wiley Jackson leaned back in his leather recliner and took in his secretary's rear assets as she glided out of his sixth floor office in the Criminal Courts Building.

"Oh, my," he said with a shake of his head. Too far he'd gotten as a black man in a white man's world to let a child like that bring him down–but, oh, the temptation.

A call from his old friend Buzz Bradley distracted him from his illicit thoughts.

Wiley's and Buzz's history went back to the University of Illinois, where, in 1956, their placement together in the Swanson Hall dormitory received wide coverage in the local press. They held the distinction of being the first interracial roommates to share a dormitory room in the university's storied history. By his junior year, Buzz was editor of the university newspaper, while Wiley became one of the university's first black law students.

Now they were both older, and maybe a little bit wiser. They were two important people in a big city–Wiley, the Cook County public defender, and Buzz, the editor of the *Northside Beat*.

Their jobs often had them butting heads now, and their interests weren't always served on the same platter. That explained why they hadn't spoken to each other in over a year.

They went far enough back that Buzz was willing, at times, to step over thin ethical lines when their interests did serve each other–like now.

"Look, Wiley, I need a favor. My reporter, Charley Hubbs, I think you know him, he needs a good lawyer."

Buzz went on to explain that Hubbs had been charged with the murder of Jimmie Dart, a drag queen whose body was found beaten and strangled at a gay bar on Halsted. The story of the search for the killer had saturated the newspapers and local TV news the past couple days.

The news caused Wiley to spill coffee on his new yellow power tie. As he wiped the stain, he said, "Yeah, I've heard about the murder, but Hubbs? I don't understand."

"I don't really understand it all myself. We're getting our attorneys on this, but the problem is, right now Charley's in custody at your courthouse awaiting a bond hearing. I'd like to see if we could get one of your best guys appointed to represent him, just for purposes of bond."

Wiley glanced around the office in search of an extra tie. "Of course. I'll get right on it."

Buzz thanked him, told him he owed him and suggested that they get together for a drink at the Billy Goat Tavern in the near future.

Wiley, in turn, promised that he'd try to do better at keeping in touch. After all, a good lawyer always collects his debts.

Wiley tapped his fingertips on the edge of his cluttered desk, as he always did when he was trying to think. The clock on the wall read 8:45 A.M. Bond court would begin in forty-five minutes. Todd "Whittler" Whittlemeyer, an over-eager, hyper-frenetic, well-meaning-but-barely-competent rookie assistant public defender was assigned to cover bond court, a place where Wiley thought he could do the least amount of harm. The Hubbs case was sure to draw a lot of local media attention, and Wiley didn't want any of that focused on Whittler. Besides, he'd promised Buzz that he'd pull out his best weapon, which meant only one person–Joshua O'Connell, his chief deputy assistant public defender.

O'Connell had toiled in the Public Defender's Office for twenty years, but not because he couldn't make it as a high-priced private defense attorney. Over the years, he'd been wooed with mega-buck offers from just about every top-notch Chicago law firm. His paycheck from the county looked like pocket change compared to what those guys were making. O'Connell was one of an almost extinct breed of public defenders whose interest was in that basic principle of justice for *all,* not just the few. In the eyes of Wiley Jackson, and of anyone who knew anything about criminal law in Chicago, Joshua O'Connell was the best defense attorney in the city, bar none.

Wiley thought O'Connell to be the *only* choice to represent Hubbs *and* the Public Defender's Office in a courtroom that would surely be a media circus, one the county's vainglorious State's Attorney Richard Bullock would no doubt try to manipulate to his advantage. There was just one problem, though, as he saw it, and that was that O'Connell was gay.

As he weighed the matter in his head, he realized that never before had he considered O'Connell's *gayness*–if that was even the proper way to characterize his homosexuality–an issue. This wasn't an ordinary case, though. A gay man had been murdered in a well-known gay bar, raising fear in the gay community. O'Connell would be aware of this and might, for obvious reasons, be hesitant to get involved–but he didn't see any other choice for the job. So he picked up the telephone and pressed the inter-office three-digit number for O'Connell.

When he heard the ring on his phone, O'Connell was in the middle of his morning ritual of rehearsing arguments he'd be making later in the day. At this particular time, he was rehearsing an argument for suppression of evidence in what he knew was a loser of a drug possession case. Chicago's finest had entered the home of his client, Willy Weed, to confiscate a boa constrictor named Bart, which a neighbor reported slithering in his backyard the day before. When the cops entered the home, they spotted a suspicious plastic baggie of white powder that field tested positive for cocaine. They arrested Willy and confiscated the suspected cocaine as well as Bart the boa, who was in Willy's kitchen having his breakfast, a plump white mouse.

Because the cocaine was found in the open, clearly within the law's "plain view" doctrine, O'Connell didn't have any argument with the cops there. That meant that, to save his client from time in one of the state penitentiaries, he'd have to argue that the evidence should be suppressed because the cops had entered Willy's *home* illegally.

He'd argue that the cops had no right to seize Bart, the boa, and, therefore, had no right to have entered the house in the first place. Checking in the *Illinois Compiled Statutes*, he found that it was perfectly legal to own a snake without a license if it is less than ten feet in length. His client claimed that Bart measured in at nine feet six inches, making him a legal snake–one that the cops had no right to grab. The only problem with the argument was that Bart had somehow slithered out of police custody and was nowhere to be found, meaning that it was Willy Weed's word against that of the cops. The judge wasn't going to buy the argument, but he'd have fun making it anyway.

The sound of his boss' strong voice so early in the morning caught him by surprise, and the request to appear in his boss' office "as soon as possible, if not earlier" had him intrigued, so he scurried to Wiley's office to find out what could possibly be so important.

As he entered Wiley's office, O'Connell first noticed the backside of his boss' tattered olive-green leather chair and cleared his throat to get his boss' attention.

Wiley spun his chair one hundred eighty degrees. With an index finger resting on his chin, he studied O'Connell for a moment, then ordered him to have a seat. Seeing O'Connell straining to find a seat, Wiley jumped in to save him. "It's over there, in the corner, with the case files on it. You can remove the files."

Following instructions, O'Connell placed the files on the floor, next to the chair, and sat down, some ten feet from his boss' desk.

Wiley's left brow turned upward. "You can move the chair closer to my desk. My bark is worse than my bite."

After scooting the chair forward, O'Connell took a moment to get comfortable and cross his legs. Sitting with his hands locked together on his lap and his gaze focused on his boss' thick fingers, which were tapping on the desk, he found himself thinking about fingernails. He'd always thought that you could tell a lot about a man by his fingernails, something he didn't find to be true for women. If the nails looked like they'd been gnawed on, it suggested that the man was either nervous or trying to quit smoking. If they were manicured, it indicated that the man was meticulous about his looks.

Wiley's nails fit into neither category. They looked over-grown, almost wild, and seemed out of balance with his otherwise well groomed, conservative presentation. The contrast suggested a complex nature to Wiley Jackson.

When Wiley stopped tapping his fingers, he cleared his throat. "Well, Josh, I expect you're wondering why I called you into my office this morning."

O'Connell was actually more surprised to hear Wiley refer to him as Josh. Nobody called him Josh–he was always O'Connell. He didn't know why or how that had come about but he accepted it, and it always surprised him to hear his first name. Anyway, he acknowledged that he was, indeed, curious. He was a little worried, but he decided not to mention that.

The reason he'd been summoned surprised O'Connell. Bond court was generally reserved for the less experienced public defenders, and he hadn't been sent down there in a long time. *Was this punishment for his taking the reins of the public defenders' union?*

When Wiley laid it all out for him, O'Connell's bottle-shaped head almost popped off his spindly neck. At first he couldn't believe that it was Charley Hubbs who'd been charged with murder. Hubbs impressed O'Connell as a fair and balanced reporter who just happened to be striking in the looks department. More troublesome was being asked to represent a man accused of killing a gay man.

Seeing that his gut instinct was right, and that O'Connell would be hesitant to take the case, Wiley pleaded. "Josh, I wouldn't be asking this of you if I didn't really need you."

"I don't–" O'Connell was at a rare loss for words. "I mean ... you know I'm gay, right?"

Wiley nodded. "Yes, but this has nothing to do with being gay or straight. It's a bond hearing. That's all."

"But it does have *everything* to do with being gay," O'Connell shot back, his face turning fiery red in a rare display of emotion. "Don't you know that the entire gay community, of which I am a member, has condemned this act as a hate crime?"

"That's pure conjecture," Wiley said, trying to calm his top lieutenant. "We have no evidence whatsoever that this murder had anything to do with the victim being gay. More to the point, we have no evidence that Charley

Hubbs committed that murder. He's innocent until proven guilty, and I know you know that, but I don't think that can be over-emphasized here."

O'Connell closed his eyes, inhaled deeply and exhaled. With his head dropped back, he opened his eyes, so that he was looking at the chipped milky white paint on the ceiling of the old courthouse. Slowly he moved his head down until his eyes met Wiley's. "You're right. You're absolutely right."

Wiley silently applauded himself. He hadn't lost his ability as a defense attorney yet. "So you'll do it? You'll take the bond hearing?"

"It's just the bond hearing, nothing more?"

Wiley confirmed that it was, that Charley Hubbs' newspaper was looking at getting its own attorneys in on the case.

"Yeah," O'Connell said, "I'll take it."

When O'Connell tapped Deputy Cordell Washington on the shoulder and motioned to let him in the lockup to see his client, Charley Hubbs, it was 9:15 A.M., fifteen minutes before bond court's scheduled start time. Although *court* time generally lagged at least thirty minutes behind *real* time, meaning that a court call that was scheduled to start at 9:30 usually wouldn't get underway until ten or later, O'Connell knew that Foxtower was a rare breed of jurist and demanded that his court call begin on time. Since there would be a standing-room-only crowd there to see Hubbs, O'Connell figured that Foxtower would call Hubbs first. That left him fifteen minutes, at most, to interview his client.

Like it or not, O'Connell knew that there was an assembly-line aspect to his job. Not only did he not get to pick and choose his clients, he also had no control over his caseload. For the most part, he was always juggling more that he could handle. In some ways he preferred it that way. If he ever stopped to think about the realities of his job, he'd probably cave in under the stress.

However, O'Connell knew that for the accused there was a lot at stake, and that no matter the constraints his job placed on him, it was his job to provide the best possible defense for his client. Bond court was the first stage in the criminal court process and often the last chance for freedom for the accused. The big prize of bond court was known as the I-bond, or personal recognizance bond–a get-out-of-jail-free trump card. If you had no money to post a bond, the alternative was a minimum of eight months in the Cook County Jail–the average length of time it took a felony case to reach trial in the Criminal Courts Building. Without the I-bond, many elected to plead guilty. The chances were good they'd get probation, which was a hell of a lot better than an eight-month sentence to the Cook County Jail, an all-inclusive resort nobody wanted to visit. That gave Foxtower a great deal of power–and he wasn't even there to judge guilt or innocence.

O'Connell just hoped that he was up to the task. As he stood at the gate of the cell that held his client, he felt a twinge of anxiety that he hadn't felt in years. In his right hand, he held a clipboard. On the clipboard was attached his bond court cheat sheet–a list of questions it would be necessary to ask of his client. Do you have any prior convictions? Do you have any family? Any friends? Any home? If so, how long have you been a member of the community? These were all factors the judge would use in weighing whether or not the accused was a serious flight risk.

O'Connell knew that an I-bond was out of the question for his client. Not only was it virtually unheard of for a murder defendant to be released on his own recognizance, it was also well-known throughout the courthouse that Foxtower held a grudge against Hubbs for a story he'd written that took him to task for releasing an accused rapist on an I-bond. No, all he could do was argue for a *reasonable* bond, meaning an amount his client would actually be able to post in order to obtain freedom pending trial.

When O'Connell first saw Charley Hubbs that morning, crouched in the corner of the courtroom's holding cell, he was surprised to find that his client didn't look like the stud puppy who'd inspired some obscene thoughts on his part in the past. Instead, he looked more like a sickly, mangy mutt. His grainy, dark brown hair was mussed, and his Oxford button-down shirt was hanging out over dirty Docker's. As he inched closer, O'Connell noticed beads of sweat dripping down Charley's unshaven face, which to him seemed odd because the temperature couldn't even be seventy degrees. "Are you okay?" he asked as he bent down to get a better look at his client.

Recognizing the voice, Charley slowly lifted his head. Through squinted eyes, he was surprised to see Joshua O'Connell. "You're my lawyer?"

O'Connell nodded. "Yeah, it looks like you're stuck with me. Just for purposes of bond hearing, though. Your paper's looking at getting its attorneys to represent you for trial."

In the two months he'd been covering the courts, Charley had never seen O'Connell in bond court. In any other circumstance, he'd consider himself fortunate to have him as counsel. A pang of guilt washed over him, which O'Connell mistook for sickness.

"You're sure you're okay? I can get a doctor for you. The hearing can be postponed."

Delay wasn't an option for Charley. "I'm just a little claustrophobic in here," he assured. "I'll be fine once I get into the courtroom."

O'Connell remained dubious but let his concern take a backseat so that he could do his job. Although he knew that Charley fully understood what the proceedings were all about, he felt obliged to explain them to him anyway, and did so, repeatedly apologizing for telling him things he already knew.

Charley's responses to the litany of questions on O'Connell's cheat sheet weren't all that favorable to him. He had no family or friends in Chicago and he'd only been living there for a couple of months. On the positive side, he had led a life free of criminal convictions and had a respectable job–though the Judge might differ on the latter point. If he had more time to prepare for the hearing, O'Connell would have tried to get Charley's boss to testify on his behalf. He'd leave it to the attorneys from the newspaper to raise that argument at another date.

When he finished questioning Charley, O'Connell put down the clipboard and examined Charley's eyes. He wanted to ask him THE QUESTION but he knew it wasn't his place to ask.

Charley read O'Connell's thoughts. "I didn't do it. I want you to know that."

O'Connell nodded. "I'm glad to hear that."

As he stood up and looked down on his client, O'Connell felt like a deadlocked jury–half wanting to believe and half unable to believe. The reality of his job was that in most cases he knew his clients *were* guilty. Those were the easy ones because it didn't bother him so much if he lost them. The tough ones were those in which he actually started to believe his own words in court. "I just hope that it's true, and that you can *prove* it's true."

In his head the night before, Charley had orchestrated his plan. Everything seemed to be in tune. Now, as the moment of truth approached, his head was filled with sour notes.

He closed his eyes and tried to get a mental picture of the courtroom. About seventy-five feet separated the judge's bench from the two heavy, wooden doors that opened up to the main hallway of the courthouse. Between them were two tables–one for the defense, one for the prosecution–and fourteen seats for the jurors. Just behind the tables there was a divider that separated the primary actors in the courtroom from the audience. A waist-high swinging gate marked the center of the divider. From there, a four-foot passageway separated ten evenly divided rows of benches for the onlookers.

When he opened his eyes, he reached with his right hand into his front pants pocket, and pulled out the note he'd scribbled the night before while cooped up in the police station lockup. As he read, beads of sweat dripped from his forehead and fell onto the paper, leaving a small trail of black ink resembling a Rorschach blot where he'd signed his name.

Charley's note was his explanation–for what, he wasn't sure. He still didn't know how he'd gotten himself into this mess.

A *mess,* that was putting it mildly. One minute he's typing a story on the conviction of a drug kingpin. The next he's being hauled away from his desk by the cops and charged with killing his neighbor, a professional drag queen named Jimmie Dart. *Yes, it's a fine mess you've gotten yourself into this time, Charley boy.*

"Hubbs ... Charles Hubbs," Deputy Washington barked from outside the lockup.

Game time.

"It's Charley," he corrected the deputy, whose smooth black head and lumbering potbelly frame made an imposing figure.

"Let's go," Washington urged, as he steered Charley in the direction of the courtroom. "No funny business now."

Organized chaos. That's how Charley viewed bond court from his seat as a reporter. He'd always wondered what it would be like to stand there, looking up at Foxtower's beady eyes and slick black mustache, charged with a crime. Now that he was there, he realized it didn't feel so good. A familiar sickly taste rose in the back of his throat. He swallowed the saliva, hoping it wouldn't come back up.

When Foxtower glanced down at him, Charley thought he detected a hint of "A-ha, I've got you now, right where I want you" in his steely eyes.

Foxtower grabbed a thin file handed to him by his clerk, Gladys. Although Gladys looked like someone's grandmother, Charley knew that she protected her judge like a grizzly protects its cubs.

When Foxtower opened the file and peeked inside, Charley saw an opening and, cautiously, turned his head.

The courtroom had drawn a capacity crowd–including a motley crew of blood-thirsty journalists, there to pick, claw and suck on the remains of one of their own.

Seated in the first row, courtroom artists from Channels 2 and 5 sketched away, hands moving at a dizzying pace, turning Charley from human being into cartoon caricature.

The TV reporters sat in the second row–the gorgeous Grace Marks and the haughty Hundley Stockwell. These two rarely stepped inside a courtroom, but still acted like they owned it.

Behind them sat the print journalists. Roger Loeper of the *Sun* sat in the third row, wearing the baggy plaid jacket with the elbow patches that he always threw on before he entered a courtroom. Douglas Gilmour of the *Daily Times,* hairpiece slightly askew, sat to Loeper's left. Seth Bronstein sat in his usual spot in the fourth row. Bronstein, of *United Wire Services,* was always quick to boast that he'd won first prize in the Illinois Press Association's spot-news reporting category the last two years' running. Meanwhile, Jonathon Barker of the *Chicago Herald* scribbled in his notebook, attempting to ignore Bronstein.

Bunched amid the journalistic pack was a gumbo-like batch of transvestites, legal eagles and court buffs. Members of BAAH, the Boys Town Alliance Against Hate, were also in the crowd, wearing hot-pink T-shirts embroidered with black lettering reading *Jimmie Dart 11/02/1993 R.I.P.*

Charley's eyes traveled to the last row of Courtroom 1012, but he still didn't see the one person he was searching for. Just as he was about to turn his head back toward the bench, the door at the back of the room opened and in slipped Danny Piper, his colleague from the *Beat*. Charley had wondered whether Piper would be there, knowing that it was quite possible, even likely, the prosecution would call him to testify. Anyway, he was glad to see him and it brought a smile to his face when he saw Piper nudge Richard Bullock, the State's Attorney, and his ample ass, for a seat in the crowded courtroom. Begrudgingly, with a look of contempt, Bullock moved over for Piper.

"Mr. Hubbs," Foxtower bellowed, trying to return the focus to his favorite place–himself. "You know who I am ... and I know who you are."

"Oh, yes. Yes, your honor," Charley uttered, his thoughts still focused elsewhere. *Where was Lizzy?* As Charley browsed the courtroom, his hope dimmed. Maybe she had doubts. Maybe she simply chickened out. Who could blame her? Maybe he shouldn't have asked her to get involved. Maybe he asked too much of her. Maybe his whole plan was doomed!

"I am not going to recuse myself," Foxtower expounded. "This is only a bond hearing." Charley had never seen the big blow-hard recuse himself once in all the times he'd been in felony bond court.

The tension in the courtroom broke when the door opened yet again. Heads turned. Exasperation was displayed like a billboard across Foxtower's face.

Charley turned toward the door to see Lizzy walk into the courtroom wearing a thin black leather jacket over a white T-shirt and painted-on jeans. She'd grown out her dyed-black hair a little so that it framed her face and highlighted her milky white skin. She was, to say the least, a sight for sore eyes. Charley's heart raced with hope again. Lizzy had come through for him. Now he needed to finally come through for her.

He surveyed the courtroom. O'Connell stood to his left. To his right was Deputy Washington. Deputy Don Larson covered his back. Charley had heard tales in the pressroom about Larson. An avid reader of *Soldier of Fortune* magazine, Larson stood only five-feet-four-inches and carried a heavy case of short-man's syndrome in his uniform. Deputy Joanie McCall stood by the divider separating the courtroom observers from the action. She appeared to be trying to get a glimpse of the drawings by the courtroom artists. A platinum-blonde grandmother from Blue Island, Deputy Joanie was as nice as they came. Charley hoped that she wouldn't take any of the blame for what he was about to do.

"Excuse me, your Honor," Charley interjected, "but may I have a moment with my public defender?"

"Of course," Foxtower said, fighting back his displeasure at having Charley steal control from him.

Charley turned to O'Connell, took his right hand and coned it around O'Connell's ear to shield his words. As he did this, he used his left hand to take the note he'd written out of his pants pocket.

"Give me your hand, O'Connell," Charley said. "Take this note. It explains everything. Do as you wish with it. You can read it to Foxtower. You can even read it to the press, if you wish. I'll leave that up to you. Oh, one last thing. You aren't going to like what I'm about to do. I know you don't want to represent me anyway. This will free you of all responsibility for me."

O'Connell glanced at the note, neatly folded, which Charley had placed in his right hand, and then turned his glance to Charley. What was going on?

Charley offered only a subtle smile to O'Connell before returning his gaze to Lizzy. As he'd instructed, she sat at the end of the last row. When her eyes met his, he gave her a quick nod.

Sweat oozed from Charley's palms and his heart raced at Indy speed. One last breath, then … he bolted, mowing down Deputy Larson like a bowling pin, hurdling over the courtroom divider, and rocketing past all of the too-stunned-to-move onlookers.

Lizzy took care of Charley's biggest worry in the courtroom–Deputy Washington–by sticking out her left foot and sending his body flying into the door as he chased after Charley.

Surprised that he'd managed to make it out of the courtroom, Charley knew he still had a daunting task ahead of him. Deputies roamed the courthouse halls like flies and stood at the exit doors. If he were to have a chance at all, he needed to reach the exit before the alarm sounded.

As he raced down the hallway, he was amazed that nobody tried to stop him. The world around him felt like it had frozen in time. Once before, he'd experienced this sensation–when he neared the end of running a marathon and a wall of people surrounded and cheered him on to the finish line. This time, the finish line was the courthouse doors and he had only about a hundred feet to go. That's when the alarm sounded.

"Shit!" There was no turning back now. Somehow he had to get past the deputies stationed at the entranceway. Most of them were retired Chicago cops and were no speed demons. Charley was banking on hope–hope that they wouldn't pull the triggers of their guns. There was good reason to believe that they wouldn't fire, and that was for the safety of others. The courthouse was always a busy place. They wouldn't take a chance of wounding, or possibly killing, innocent people just to stop one man. Or would they?

Joanie's radio call came just as Charley was speeding past the deputies stationed at the door. The deputies chased him out the door and yelled orders to stop. Charley kept running down the long stairwell. They didn't fire a single shot.

Lizzy had parked his rusty, red Hyundai Excel in the fifteen-minute meter spot directly across from the courthouse, just as she'd been instructed to do. The doors were left unlocked and the key was in the ignition.

As Charley turned the key, his foot trembled over the gas pedal. The motor roared and he forced his foot down on the pedal. The car chugged and chugged and then stalled.

"Shit!" Battles with his car were nothing new for Charley. Turning his head toward the window, he viewed a wave of deputies coming his way. "Come on, baby." With eyes closed, he turned the ignition again. The motor roared.

"Thank you! Now come on, baby!" He floored the gas pedal and the car jumped and chugged and slowly gained speed. Soon Charley found himself racing at fifty miles per hour through the city streets. The car, like him, seemed to be running on pure adrenaline. Sirens wailed in the distance but there was no sign of the cops in the rearview mirror.

After weaving in and out of traffic and neighborhood side streets for about five minutes, Charley slowed the car down as he turned it into a U-Store-It rental storage lot. With a quick scan, he determined there was nobody in the vicinity.

After he stopped the car, he opened the glove compartment. Sitting on top of a pile of maps and the owner's manual was a key, marked with the number 201.

When he found the storage locker with the number that matched that on the key, he got out of the car, inserted the key into the locker, turned the key, and lifted the sliding door. He then hopped back in the car and drove in.

The locker was barely wide enough to fit his compact car. Once the car was parked, he caught his breath, got out of the car and closed the sliding door from the inside.

His watch showed the time to be 11:05 A.M. Lizzy wouldn't be coming until the next morning–if she came at all. Leaving him in the cold, dark storage locker for eternity might just be her way of exacting revenge.

Courtroom 1012 looked like a hurricane had ripped through it.

Washington picked himself up off the floor. There was a bump on his head, which had collided with the door.

Larson lay flat on the floor, staring at the stars floating above his eyes.

Foxtower silenced the chattering courtroom by rapping on his gavel. All heads turned to the bench.

Foxtower glared down at poor old O'Connell as if he were the one on trial. "How do you let your client get away with such behavior, such utter contempt for the court?"

O'Connell felt like telling Foxtower the truth–that he didn't even want this case, that he fought with his supervisor just an hour ago because he didn't think he could fairly represent the accused. Instead, he told him the other truth. "Believe me, I knew nothing, had nothing to do with what just occurred here, your Honor. He just handed me this note."

"Let me see that," Foxtower ordered.

"I don't know if I can do that. I haven't even opened it myself. It could be incriminating."

"Mr. O'Connell, your client has already committed a criminal act in my presence," Foxtower huffed. "I don't see how anything he wrote on that piece of paper could be any more incriminating."

"I guess he did say that I could read this to you, as well as to the press." Each member of the press now came to attention.

"Well, then, go on, damnit," Foxtower yapped, "read it!"

Carefully unfolding the paper, O'Connell skimmed through the note before clearing his throat. "The note is addressed to myself, Judge Foxtower and all members of the press who are in attendance. It says, 'By the time you read this, I will either be back in custody or free on my own recognizance. Obviously, my hope is for the latter. I do intend to face the charges that have been brought against me, but not until I am able to prove my innocence. I cannot do that from a jail cell. I declare to you all that I am an innocent man. I believe that what I have done, or attempted to do, will allow me to prove that to all of you. I apologize for any problems that my actions have caused, but I do believe them to be necessary. Sincerely…'"

O'Connell flashed a sheepish eye upon Foxtower. "That's it. It looks like he signed it, but the ink's smeared where his signature should be."

PART I
Season of Futility

Wrigley Field is a Peter Pan of a ballpark. It has never grown up and it has never grown old. Let the world race on–they'll still be playing day baseball in the friendly confines of Wrigley Field, outfielders will still leap up against the vines and the Cubs ... well, it's the season of hope. This could be the Cubbies' year."

– E.M Swift

Chapter 1
Die-hards

Two months earlier

The ivy clinging to the outfield wall shimmered in the warm September breeze. Harry Caray waved his microphone in the air. The shirtless post-frat party boys and the pretty girls clad in halter tops swayed back and forth in unison in the Wrigley Field bleachers. They punched out their fingers in tandem "One … two … three strikes you're out."

This was Charley's first seventh-inning stretch at Wrigley Field, and it made him feel like a kid again. For a moment, he was back on the Little League field playing first base for the Davenport Tigers chanting "Aaaaay, battuh. Aaaaaay, battuh. Sssswwwwiiiing, battuh."

Those were the days when he'd rush home from school, dump the books, pick up the baseball and bat, head out into the yard, and play, alone, tossing the ball in the air, mimicking his heroes. Ernie Banks. Billy Williams. Ron Santo. Always he dreamed that one day he'd play on that same field, stand in that batter's box, and pick up that dirt and rub it into his hands.

As a kid, Charley had only heard the sounds of the ballpark crackling through his transistor radio. Now, sitting in the left field bleachers, six rows back of the three hundred sixty-feet marker on the ivy-covered outfield wall, he understood why fans kept coming back there, even though the Cubs hadn't won a World Series since 1908. There was more than just a game on that field. There was a ballpark that locked in memories like a time capsule just waiting to release them each time a fan walked through the turnstile.

When he made his first pilgrimage to Wrigley Field, the Phillies were in town for a three-game series. After a flirtation with first place in early June, the Cubs had sunk to their usual depths by early September. Entering the game, they trailed the first place Phillies by eleven games with only twelve games left in the regular season. By the time the game ended, the Cubs had been mathematically eliminated from contention, losing twelve to three, despite Harry Caray's phlegm-spewing plea of "Let's get some rohnnns!"

As the grounds crew began to roll out the tarp over the infield, the bleacher crowd spilled out onto Sheffield and Clark and into the taverns in Wrigleyville. Charley, however, didn't budge from his seat–his troubles could wait a while longer. At that moment, it didn't matter that he was jobless, homeless and had no idea where he was going, what he was going to do or how he even got there. There would be another time to figure that all out. Right now he just wanted to breathe in all of the memories that had evaded him for so long.

Twenty minutes elapsed before a security guard noticed him still sitting in his bleacher seat, gazing out at the field. "Hey, buddy, you've got to pack it up. Park's closed."

The words shook Charley out of his trance. He nodded, but didn't move his gaze from the ballpark. A couple of moments of awkward silence passed. Then he turned his attention to the guard. "Sorry. I guess I didn't realize I was the last one here."

As if he was under a hypnotic spell, he stood and moved down the winding ramp out of the bleacher section. Stepping out of the ballpark at the corner of Waveland and Sheffield, the streets he'd never been on seemed familiar, like a neighborhood from his childhood. Across the street, a tavern named Murphy's Bleachers had seemed to swallow in much of the bleacher crowd that had left the game.

Turning right, he walked south on Sheffield one block, to Addison, and then he took another right turn and walked another block, to Clark. There, he looked up at the stadium. WRIGLEY FIELD: HOME OF CHICAGO CUBS, the giant red sign read. A picture of that image once sat on his desk at the *San Francisco Star*. Now, like everything else he possessed, it was packed away in one of the many boxes that filled his rusting Hyundai Excel.

Setting out without so much as a plan as to where he was headed, Charley glided in that dream-like state. Turning right on Clark, he wandered past a dilapidated Mexican restaurant and an old-time tavern, and then past a music club called Metro. Just past Metro, he espied the Ginger Man tavern. A sign outside read LIVE CLASSICAL MUSIC AFTER EVERY CUBS GAME.

This place seemed to suit his mood. Sitting on a stool outside the door was a baldheaded man whose bulging biceps seemed to stretch his thick black leather biker jacket to the seams.

"Nice day, huh?" Charley said, looking around and seeing nobody else wearing jackets.

"Got ID," the bouncer said. Charley nodded and handed over his driver's license. The bouncer studied the ID for longer than seemed necessary to check a birth date before he looked up at Charley. "California, huh? I lived in Berkeley many years ago. Lot of fog there."

"Yeah, I just came from there. I arrived in Chicago today."

"Well you found the right place." The bouncer's affability belied his rough outer shell. "Come on in. You're our first customer of the evening."

Inside there were three violinists in the corner of the bar, playing to nobody but themselves. They reminded Charley of the musicians that continued to play while the Titanic sank.

The walls of the bar were decorated with an eclectic mix of auto racing memorabilia, old movie stills and antique paintings. Behind the bar, a woman sat on a stool, reading Albert Camus' *The Stranger*.

After straddling up to the bar, Charley studied the woman. He couldn't say she was his type–but he couldn't say she wasn't. She looked like nothing he'd seen before. Caribbean blue eyes stood out against pure white skin and short dyed-black hair. Skin-tight black jeans wrapped a nice bottom. A black half-T-shirt, emblazoned with the words LICENSE TO SPILL, exposed a pierced navel.

Lifting her head from her book, she looked Charley's way. "You're new here," she said.

"Yes," said Charley, adjusting himself in his stool. "I just sat down."

"No, you're new to this bar. I've never seen you in here before."

Charley nodded. "As a matter of fact, I'm new to Chicago. I've been in the city now for … let me see…" After giving a false glance at his watch, he returned his eyes to the woman behind the bar. "It's been a little over five hours. I got into town just in time to catch the Cubs game."

The bartender shook her head as if she'd heard this same wretched tale hundreds of times before. "Oh, no, please don't tell me you're one of them."

"One of whom?"

"The die-hards," the bartender spit out, like she was coughing up a hairball. "One of those nuts who follows the Cubs like they're a religion, waiting for a championship like it is the coming of Christ. It's crazy. I see 'em all the time. It's a sickness, an infectious disease that's being spread across the country by WGN."

Taken slightly aback but also intrigued by this spitfire, Charley replied, "Guilty as charged."

The bartender continued shaking her head, as she flipped a bar rag over her right shoulder and then positioned her hands on her waist. "I think all Cubs fans are in dire need of a lobotomy."

"Sorry." He wasn't sure what he was apologizing for but that didn't seem to matter. "Can't do anything about it. It's in my blood. I hope you won't hold it against me. I could really use a beer right now."

The bartender steadied her gaze on Charley. "No, I won't hold it against you," she finally said after completing her eye exam and deciding she liked what she saw. "If I did that, I'd never get any business in here. What can I get you?"

"Whatever's on tap." His eyes wandered.

"We've got twenty different beers on tap here. You'll have to narrow it down a little."

"Oh, well, then, what would you recommend?" Charley's mind seemed to be stuttering.

"How 'bout a Honker's Ale."

A puzzled look came to Charley's face. "Honker's Ale?"

"It's brewed in Chicago, by Goose Island Brewery. Try it. If you're going to be a Chicagoan, you're going to have to start drinkin' like one."

"Okay. A Honker's Ale it'll be."

The bartender studied Charley some more as she poured his beer from the tap. "So, Die-hard," she said as she set down a coaster on the bar and placed the beer in front of him, "do you have a name?"

"Yes. It's Charley. Charley Hubbs."

"Hubbs ... hmmm ... that means you're a victim of the ex-Cub factor."

"What's that supposed to mean?"

"You share the same last name as an ex-Cub–Kenny Hubbs. He won rookie-of-the-year for the Cubs in 1962. He died two years later in a plane crash. Tragic story, actually."

"For someone who dislikes the Cubs so much, you sure know an awful lot about them."

"I don't really dislike the Cubs. What I don't like is the silly mystique that seems to surround them–the blind loyalty of their fans. My father was one of the die-hards. He was actually one of the old Bums, the Bleacher Bums. True story. That's why I know so much about the Cubs. I learned it all from my father. The problem was, I think my father cared more about the Cubs than he did about me. Imagine that, caring more about a baseball team than about your only daughter. It's pathetic, really."

"You seem to have come out all right, as far as I can tell." Charley liked this girl, despite her distaste for Cubs fans. "You know my name. I just realized I still don't know yours."

"It's Marla. Marla Collins."

"You're kidding me, right? Your name's not really Marla Collins." He flushed with memories of juvenile lust. Marla Collins had been a ballgirl for the Cubs in the early 1980s and a favorite of Cubs' broadcaster Harry Caray, who had an eye for beautiful women. Marla lost her job with the Cubs organization after she posed nude for *Playboy*.

"No. That was just a test to see if you really are a die-hard. My name's Elizabeth Zapler. Most people just call me Lizzy, or T.L."

"T.L.?"

"Short for Thin Lizzy. After the band, you know–'The Boys Are Back In Town.'" She played a little air guitar for emphasis.

"Well, Lizzy, or T.L., you're certainly one of a kind, and I mean that as a compliment."

"Compliment taken. Looks like you could use another Honker's."

"Sure. Why not?" Charley paused for a moment and considered what he was about to do. "Lizzy, I know I just met you, but I'm kind of in a bind here.

I need a place to stay and, quite frankly, you're the only person I know in Chicago."

"Well, Charley Hubbs, you're more daring than I took you for. Are you asking what I think you're asking?"

Charley choked on his beer. "No," he coughed. "You think I'm asking to stay … with you? Believe me, I'm not that presumptuous at all. I just need help finding an apartment, and I thought you might have some ideas on where I could start. I'm kind of lost here."

"Boy, just when a girl thinks she's got a hot one, caution is thrown to the wind and stops the flames from spreading." Lizzy made it seem as if she were teasing Charley, but she was disappointed that this mysterious stranger who'd found his way into her bar had not been presumptuous. She thought he was kind of cute. He had a good face and warm, thinking brown eyes. "Check out the *Reader*. That's the newspaper piled up in that corner by the window. That's where everybody looks to find an apartment in Chicago."

"I'll do that. Thanks, Lizzy."

Resting her elbow on the bar, Lizzy watched Charley walk like a rookie ballplayer stepping onto the field for the first time. A faint smile bloomed across her face as she thought of him wearing nothing but a cowboy hat and chaps. A fleeting forbidden thought.

When Charley returned to his barstool, he laid the paper down in front of him. As he started to turn the first page, Lizzy blurted, "Section Four."

"Huh?"

"Section Four. That's where you'll find the apartment listings."

"Oh, thanks. I seem to be saying that a lot–thanks, that is. You've been very nice to me."

"Well, you look like a lost puppy, and I'm a sucker for puppies, especially lost ones."

They exchanged timid smiles. For a moment they just took each other in. Neither one had any idea where this was going. That didn't seem to faze Charley, who'd grown accustomed to being lost. However, Lizzy needed something more than a blank map. "So … do you even have any idea where you want to live?"

Charley laughed. "Not a clue. Do you want to tell me?"

Placing both hands on the edge of the bar, Lizzy peered into Charley's eyes. "Chicago's broken down into neighborhoods," she said as if on autopilot. "Where you're at now is called the Wrigleyville neighborhood. But it's also called Lakeview, which is what it was originally known as before the yuppies started moving in and started calling it Wrigleyville, after its most famous landmark. Lakeview extends much farther than Wrigleyville. South of Lakeview is the Lincoln Park neighborhood and north of Lakeview is Andersonville and Ravenswood. To the west of us is an up-and-coming neighborhood, Southport. As far as you're concerned, I'd limit your search to those neighborhoods. I assume you want to stay close to Wrigley?"

"Yes. I ... I don't know. Actually, I never really thought about it--until now. I suppose if I was drawn here by Wrigley Field, I should probably take that as a sign I was meant to live here as well."

When Lizzy then asked an innocent question about rent, Charley offered up more questions than answers. "I don't know, I think I can afford five hundred a month–maybe. I don't even have a job at this point, and I don't have much left in my bank account after–"

"After what?"

"Never mind. It's a long story and not worth getting into."

"Well, Charley, you're jobless, almost penniless and it's starting to sound like you're carrying some heavy baggage. You're every girl's wet dream."

Charley chuckled uneasily. "So can I afford to live around here or not?" This was Charley's way of getting back to the point while sidestepping issues he didn't care to walk into right now and wasn't even sure he could answer.

"Yes, but you're not going to find much in the range of five hundred-a-month. A one-bedroom is out of the question. But you can probably get a studio in one of the older buildings for that much."

"Sounds delightful."

"Look for yourself. Here's a pen. Just circle anything in the neighborhoods I mentioned that fits your criteria, which in your case is pretty narrow. You won't find much for that rent, but you will find some. While you're doing that, I've got to get back to my job. I've got a customer down at the end of the bar who seems to be getting a bit impatient."

A gangly creature with a scraggly beard sat at the opposite end of the bar, jotting notes onto a pad of paper. There was something about him that made Charley do a double take. Charley was unable to put his finger on it. Had he seen this man before? There were so many things he couldn't remember. Thoughts about the strange man at the bar soon faded and Charley set himself to the task at hand–starting a new life.

When he next glanced at his watch, it was 10:30 P.M. The bar, though by no means packed, had filled in. All of the stools at the bar were now occupied and the benches and chairs around all of the tables were also taken. The age of the crowd appeared to be mid-twenties to early thirties, which put him at the upper end of the age scale but not completely out of his element.

Although the bar was busy, Lizzy made time to check in on Charley every once in a while and keep his mug full. He figured he'd drunk about six pints, which was the most alcohol he'd consumed in a long time–enough to give him a pretty good buzz.

Before closing Section Four for the night, he took one last look at the apartment listings. Initially, he'd circled about a dozen places that had some potential, meaning he could afford them. He narrowed the list to three that he'd call first thing tomorrow.

When she saw Charley folding up the *Reader,* Lizzy broke away from another customer and moved over to him.

"Any success?" She clasped her hands together behind her back, lifted her shoulders and moved her head close to his.

"Potentially. Who knows what these places will actually look like, but I did circle a few I could probably swing."

"Good. So what about tonight?"

"I thought I'd find my car and pass out in it. It won't take much. I haven't had this much to drink in some time."

"That's ridiculous," Lizzy declared with raised brows. "Sleep in your car? And then you're going to search for an apartment looking like a bum? No. Not acceptable. You'll stay with me for the night. I'm off in half an hour. Wait for me." She couldn't believe she was actually trying to convince a guy to stay the night with her–a first for her. Usually she had to fight them off, just one of the fringe benefits of bartending.

Placing his elbows on the bar, Charley stretched his hands over both sides of his face. He breathed deeply, lifting his head back without moving his hands so that his hands came together as if in prayer under his chin. Lifting a brow, he said, "Okay. But only if you promise you'll let me make you dinner once I'm settled into my own apartment."

"Deal. Half an hour."

Lizzy turned and reached for the coffee pot and a cup. "Drink this. You've had enough Honker's for tonight."

After she poured the coffee, she advanced to Henry, the bartender scheduled to close for the night. She whispered in his ear, "Henry, do you think you can handle this on your own if I take off a little early?"

A scan of the bar and Henry nodded. "I think so. Yeah, I'm sure I can. It looks like it's starting to die down a bit. They should be moving on to bed or to Smart Bar pretty soon."

"Thanks, Henry." Lizzy gave Henry a peck on the right cheek, something she hadn't done previously in the eight months the two of them had been working together. Henry smirked and lifted his brows in wonderment.

"I owe you one," Lizzy said with a gushing smile.

After a perfunctory round of taking care of tabs and cleaning a little around the bar, she dashed into the ladies room, locking the door behind her. Looking into the mirror above the sink, she shook her head and took a deep breath. Shrugging, she laughed at herself, and moved her head closer to the mirror to touch up her lipstick. Satisfied, she unlocked the door and pranced back out into the bar.

Lizzy found Charley where she'd left him, clutching his cup in both palms and staring down into the blackness of the coffee. A tap on his right shoulder gave him a bit of a startle.

"What's a girl got to do to get a die-hard started?"

Charley smiled and returned the volley. "You've already juiced me up with all those Honker's. Don't tell me that you've got jumper cables, too?"

"You're pretty quick, for a die-hard," Lizzy quipped. "Get off of that stool. We're leaving this dive."

The cool night air felt good on Charley's skin and helped to sober him up a bit. As they crossed Clark, Lizzy took his left hand in her right. Charley didn't hesitate and they continued walking east a few blocks until Lizzy stopped in front of a rehabbed, red brick three-flat. "Well, this is it. This is where I live."

Pulling her keys out of her purse, she opened the door to the building and pointed up the stairs. "All the way to the top," she directed.

Lizzy let herself into the apartment, expecting Charley would follow. When he didn't budge, she smirked. "Are you coming in or not?"

"Yes, of course." Charley entered apprehensively, uncertain that he was ready for what might lie ahead.

Lizzy caught the wariness in Charley's eyes. "It's not much, but it's what I call home. Sorry if it's a little untidy. I wasn't really expecting company."

"It's very nice," Charley said, thinking that it was, indeed, very nice. "It fits you." Almost immediately his eyes zoomed in on a framed photo of a young girl in a Cubs hat sitting in the Wrigley bleachers with an older man. "That's you and…"

"My father," Lizzy jumped in. "That was one of the last times I went to Wrigley. I was thirteen at the time. My father died a year later. He never did see the one thing he lived his whole life for."

"What's that?"

"The Cubs win a World Series."

Charley nodded, as he scanned the room and observed that there were books practically everywhere, even on the floor. "You must read a lot."

"Yes," Lizzy said, casting her eyes about. "I keep telling myself I should donate some of the books I've already read, but I can never seem to part with them. It's like, once I've read a book, it becomes a part of me–and I guess a part of this apartment, too." Her words faded and there were a couple moments of silence between them before she asked, "So, can I get you anything? A drink?"

"No, I think I've had more than enough to drink tonight. Thank you for the offer. And thank you again for letting me crash here tonight. I must seem like an utter fool to you."

By now Lizzy had surmised that if anything was to happen, she'd have to make it happen. Although she preferred her men to be the aggressors, she didn't mind role reversal at times. This was one of those times. Interjecting with a weak impersonation of Mr. T, she said, "Yes, and I pity the fool who takes up with me." Lowering her eyes, she took a bold step forward and corralled Charley's hands.

For a couple of moments they just gazed into each other's eyes, until Lizzy lifted her chin with an open mouth. When their lips finally met, Charley pulled Lizzy into him. Lizzy's knees buckled with the force of Charley's arms. The hours of flirtatious gamesmanship spilled out in that one passionate kiss. Acting on instinct, Lizzy's fingers found Charley's shirt buttons. In a slow, rhythmic dance they moved from one button, down to the next, until they hit bottom and the fingers of both hands took over, ripping Charley's jersey out of its cozy resting place. Pressing her concealed breasts against the bare skin of Charley's stomach made her gasp in delight and she slid her hands down so that they could feel the volcanic heat emanating from below belt line. With a deft motion, Lizzy freed the button at the top of Charley's jeans and latched onto the zipper handle. Dizzily she began to pull down when Charley turned off the heat.

"I'm sorry, Lizzy," he said, backing away. "I can't do this. Not right now, anyway."

Rejection was hard for Lizzy to swallow. She'd rarely experienced it, and whenever things didn't work out the way she presupposed, she had a tendency to blame herself. "Did I come on too strong? Or do you just not find me attractive or sexy?"

"Oh, my God, trust me, it's neither of those," Charley assured. "I've been attracted to you since I laid eyes on you. I just don't think sleeping together is the right thing. I need a friend right now. Sex, love, all that other stuff, I don't think I'm ready for it."

"Can't we still be friends and have a little romp in the sack, too?" She was only half-joking.

"Trust me, Lizzy, I'm a head case," Charley confessed. "You were right when you guessed that I'm carrying some baggage. I don't want to burden you with the extra luggage I'm carrying right now. When I'm ready, I promise, you'll be the first to know."

"I guess that means I'm on stand-by," Lizzy said, her frown turning to a slight smile as she looked Charley in the eyes and lifted her brows. "To think, I dug out the jumper cables for nothing."

Charley leaned over and kissed her lightly on the forehead. "You go to sleep. I'll make myself a bed out here on your couch. I've got a busy day of apartment-hunting ahead of me tomorrow."

Chapter 2

'69

Charley felt a weight on his chest that he knew wasn't there when he passed out on the couch the night before. Easing his eyelids open, through a bloodshot haze he glimpsed two turquoise ovals putting him under the microscope, making sure that he was good enough for her. The heavy cushion of white fur that had settled itself on his upper torso didn't like most of the men she brought home.

Lizzy slipped in from the bedroom, wearing a gray half T-shirt and a matching pair of gray shorts. "I see you've made acquaintance with Camus." She stretched her arms in the air tantalizingly, not at all shy about showing what lie underneath.

"She didn't really introduce herself. She kind of just made herself at home on my chest."

"It's he, not she. He must like you if he feels that comfortable with you. He won't sit on top of me. I think he prefers men. I've often suspected he was gay."

"You named him after Albert Camus, the French existentialist—I noticed you were reading one of his books last night when I walked into the bar."

"You're very observant. That's a good thing. Most men aren't. Yes, Camus is my favorite author. Have you read any of his work?" Lizzy liked a man who could match her intellectually.

Charley told her he'd read *The Plague* and *The Stranger*, two of

Camus' better-known works, in graduate school but found them kind of depressing and went on to admit to being an Ernest Hemingway admirer.

"And Hemingway's not depressing?" Lizzy retorted.

"I can't argue that Hemingway didn't have a family history of depression and suicide. It's his writing style that grabs me. He's sometimes criticized for writing short, choppy sentences, but that's the way he was taught to write. He was a journalist before he was ever a novelist, and that strongly influenced his style of writing. I guess I appreciate what he did because, like him, I come from a journalism background."

Intrigued, Lizzy prodded for more information. "You studied journalism?"

"I worked for a newspaper in California." Charley was surprised that he could talk about his past. "I've been out of work now for a few weeks. I don't know if I can go back to it or not."

"Charley, you're full of surprises." She hoped she'd hear more.

"You don't know the half of it."

"Should I be afraid?" Lizzy raised a brow. There was good reason to be afraid, but Lizzy didn't see that side of it. The mystery only made Charley more desirable to her.

"Probably," Charley chuckled. Assessing her in the morning light, he admired her curvy body and natural beauty all over again.

Lizzy noticed that Charley was mentally undressing her–and she liked it. After the previous night's rejection, she needed a dose of flattery, even if it was unspoken.

Blind to Lizzy's needs, Charley inadvertently splashed cold water on her all over again by shifting focus from her. "Say, what time is it?" he asked.

"It's almost ten," Lizzy snapped.

Women were alien creatures to Charley. He couldn't understand them. They made him feel awkward and shy. When he became uncomfortable, he tended to avoid them–like now. Instead of talking about last night, he asked for the phone.

Lizzy pointed to the wall phone next to the dinner table, underneath the Friskies cat calendar. Rejected again. She'd hoped he'd drop his apartment search and bunk with her–at least until she got tired of him, something that always happened. What was it that attracted her to him? Yes, he was good-looking, in a preppy schoolboy kind of way—and he was intelligent and mysterious. But why had he shot her down? No man had ever turned her away—ever. She didn't know how to take it. *Was he gay?* She hoped not. There was something about him. But what was it? Curiosity? Lust? Whatever it was, she didn't want to let him go just yet.

"Thanks," Charley said, as he rose from the couch, not bothering to put his jeans on over his boxers.

Watching Charley move, Lizzy sighed. His grainy, thick brown hair was mussed from sleeping but that, along with his dark, unshaven face, only made him wilder, more appealing. For the first time, she also got a good glimpse of his body, his smooth, six-pack stomach and strong runner's legs. When he gave her that Tom Cruise smile as he walked by, she felt her body quiver. For her own good, she stopped herself from saying anything more. "Make yourself at home," she said. "I'm going to take a shower."

The chill of the water on her bare skin felt good but she couldn't rinse away the feeling of sensual desire she felt toward Charley.

Stepping out of the shower, she combed her wet hair back, slipped on a bathrobe and walked back out into the kitchen, where she found Charley's ear still attached to the phone.

Lizzy opened the refrigerator and pulled out a carton of eggs, a loaf of bread and a milk carton. Opening a cabinet, she pulled out a frying pan that almost had cobwebs on it from disuse. She couldn't believe she was actually making breakfast for a man. This was a first for her. June Cleaver, eat your heart out. She shook her head in disbelief.

"That's 12:30," Charley said into the phone. "Bradley Place Apartments. Great. I'll see you then."

After Charley hung up the phone, he turned to Lizzy and smiled as she invitingly approached with a plate of scrambled eggs and toast.

"I hope you like eggs. I'm not much of a cook and this was about all that I had in the fridge."

"Of course. You really didn't have to go to all of this trouble, though."

"It wasn't any trouble. In fact," she toyed as she eyed her wristwatch, "it took an entire five minutes out of my day."

"Well, then, thank you for spending that five minutes on making me breakfast. I'm actually starving." The last meal Charley had eaten was a Chicago-style hot dog at the ballpark eighteen hours ago.

Lizzy sat at the table, resting her chin on the palm of her right hand as she watched Charley devour his breakfast. "So, how many apartments are you seeing today? It sounded like you were pretty busy on the phone."

Charley stopped his fork in mid-flight between his plate and mouth. "Two."

"Two? That's it–just two?"

"I called all three," Charley explained. "The three places I'd narrowed it down to last night. One was already taken. I've got appointments to see the other two."

"Where are these two apartments?"

"One's here in Wrigleyville, on Bradley Place. Do you know where that is?"

"Sure, it's just a couple of blocks east of here. Where's the other place?"

"That's in Lincoln Park–on Lincoln Park West. Apparently it's right across from a zoo. The rental agent for that complex seemed very friendly. She was quite helpful."

"Yes, I know that street, too." Lincoln Park West was a rather exclusive street. Five hundred dollars might get him a garage space. "That sounds *great*." She paused to gather her thoughts. "You know, Charley, if neither of these places works out, you *can* stay here until you find something." There, she said it. Not too pushy. Not overly committal.

"Thanks," Charley said as he cleaned up the last of the scrambled eggs. "I'll take that under advisement. I owe you an awful lot, you know. I still have to ask one more thing of you, though."

"What's that?"

"I could really use a shower."

Lizzy smiled. Even though her mystery man had at times treated her as if she was invisible, he still had a strange charm about him. "Of course, there are extra towels in the hall closet, outside of the bathroom."

While Charley showered, Lizzy dug through her dresser drawer stuffed with half T-shirts until she found the right one. This one she hadn't worn in some time, but it seemed to fit her mood today. She pulled it over her shoulders and looked at herself in the mirror. The number sixty-nine in bold letters stood out on her chest. A smile of great satisfaction exploded on her face.

Moments later Charley jumped out of the bathroom wearing nothing but a towel around his waist. "You don't have any hot water," he said, shivering. Glimpsing Lizzy's shirt, he lifted his brows and smirked. "You really do like to tease, don't you?"

"What's that supposed to mean?" She knew exactly what it was supposed to mean, but she wanted him to say it–yearned for him to say it.

"Your T-shirt ... it's somewhat sexually suggestive, don't you think?"

"I suppose it could be interpreted that way." This was a role Lizzy had played many times before, but this time it seemed to be more fun than usual. "But that's not why I wear it. To me, it's a reminder. As a die-hard, you should know that sixty-nine has another meaning for Cubs fans. The collapse. The New York Mets. The curse. The Cubs were supposed to win it all in '69. They had an insurmountable lead and managed to blow it. So I wear this T-shirt as a reminder of that for people like you."

Lizzy playfully turned around to expose the back of the T-shirt and its message, which read, "The best way to screw with a Cubs fan."

Charley shook his head, smiled and chuckled. "Lizzy, you're something else." He meant that, in a good way.

"You don't know the half of it," Lizzy toyed as she slid her fingers down Charley's bare chest and came to the knot of the towel at his waist. "I could still show you, though." She lifted a brow.

Charley sensed a rise under the towel but didn't act on it. "I've already taken one cold shower this morning. I don't know if I can take another."

Disappointment showed in Lizzy's eyes. A gentle touch of two fingers on her lips helped ease her hurt. "Lizzy, I've got an appointment to see an apartment in a little over half an hour. I've got to get dressed and get a move on."

"I was just having fun," she lied. The truth was she wanted to pull the knot on that towel and throw herself at him. "I have to open up at the Ginger Man today. In fact, I was just out the door. Stop by the bar later this afternoon. Let me know how things went."

After glancing at the ground, she lifted her head and kissed Charley on his right cheek. "Promise me that you'll stop by the bar later today."

"I promise," Charley said, meaning it.

"Lock up as you leave." Lizzy felt she could trust him, even though she didn't really know him.

Standing on the cold tile of the bathroom floor, wearing nothing but his briefs, Charley reflected on the last twelve hours. He *could* remember them. That was a good sign. Maybe he was healing. Part of his life, however, remained an empty slate. He could remember his childhood, college and work—everything up to the time of the accident. After that it all became cloudy. Part of his life had become a mystery to him.

He tried to shrug it off as he reached down and picked up the jeans and polo shirt he'd worn the previous day. Ballgame sweat and barroom smoke permeated the clothes. Ordinarily he would have tossed them aside and changed into something clean, but he was in a strange woman's apartment and the rest of his wardrobe was packed in his car several blocks away. His life, as he knew it, was in that car.

Charley was almost out the door when he realized he'd forgotten his apartment list. On a napkin, he'd jotted down *Lincoln Park West Apartments 11:15–Apartment Manager Darlene Halbersham. Bradley Place 12:30–Ring doorbell for manager.*

Before he left, he glanced around Lizzy's apartment, making sure he hadn't forgotten something. Not that there was anything to forget. He came with nothing and he was leaving with nothing.

As he walked through the quiet tree-lined streets surrounding Wrigley Field, he thought how different it seemed than when he'd walked on them the evening before. In the course of eighteen hours the neighborhood had been transformed, its high-energy, rhythmic post-game pulse slowing to a sleepy Muzak crawl. When he reached Clark and saw the Ginger Man tavern across the street, his thoughts turned back to Lizzy. He had to do something special for her, but at the same time, he didn't want to lead her on. He knew he could fall for a girl like Lizzy. But first things first. Right now, he had to start a new life.

When he found his car fifteen minutes later, he also found a ticket lodged underneath the windshield. He'd illegally parked on a street designated for cleaning that day. The fine for his transgression was one hundred dollars. His new life was off to a less than rousing kick off.

Tossing the ticket onto the passenger seat, he got in his car and inserted the key into the ignition. Before he could turn it, he blacked out. He'd had these spells before and this one, like the others, quickly passed. When he regained consciousness, he felt a bit lightheaded but otherwise felt fine. The spell had lasted only about a minute or two. He took a couple minutes more to regain his composure before he felt it was safe to drive and turned the ignition. The brain file of things he wasn't ready to deal with had a new addition.

Searching for an apartment helped Charley forget what had just happened. The first apartment he went to view had been rented before he got there, so he was crossing his fingers for better luck when he arrived at the Bradley Place Apartments, a World War I-era red brick three-story complex wrapped around a nondescript courtyard.

On the west side of the building, he located a sign for a rental office, which pointed down a short stairwell. Following the sign down the stairs, he came to an unmarked wooden door. He rang the doorbell but got no answer, so he tried knocking. Still there was no response. Looking around, he didn't see any signs of life. Shaking his head, he hiked back to the front of the complex. To his surprise, he found the front door unlocked and he strolled inside.

The building's interior appeared desolate and dark for one o'clock in the afternoon. In the dim light, Charley glimpsed what looked like a ghost headed toward him. Shaking his head, he tried to adjust his eyes. As the apparition neared, it transformed into a tall, skeleton-thin man in his early twenties whose pale skin and buggy eyes were highlighted by black clothing and a shaved head. Charley stopped in his tracks and watched drop-jawed as the mysterious creature walked right by him, as if he were invisible.

"Excuse me!" Charley barked in a desperate plea for attention.

At the sound of Charley's words, the man stopped, twirled around in a slow, deliberate motion, and gazed at Charley.

"Can you tell me where I can find the rental agent for these apartments?" Charley asked.

The question was met by the man with a slight turn of the head and a contemplative eye, like he was mulling over whether Charley would taste better with catsup or Dijon mustard.

Exasperated, Charley tried again, this time pronouncing each word deliberately, as if he were speaking to a deaf person. "I'm look-ing … for the per-son … who shows … the apart-ments. Do you know … where I might … find him?"

"Oh, are you here to see the apartment that's for rent?" Charley nodded anxiously. "You were supposed to go to the rental office. There's a sign outside."

"I did. There was no answer there when I rang the doorbell. I also knocked, but nobody answered the door."

"That's because I hadn't gotten there yet."

Charley shook his head in disbelief. "So, *you're* showing me the apartment?"

"Yes. You should have said that was why you were here."

Dumbfounded, Charley glared. Just as he was ready to explode, he cut his own fuse, reminding himself why he was there. He *needed* an apartment.

As Charley followed his guide, he asked him if he'd been the person he'd spoken to on the phone.

"No."

"Whom did I speak to then?"

"That would be someone from the real estate agency. I just show apartments for them. I replied to a flier that was posted in the building. They give me a slight break on my rent for doing this job for them."

Unsolicited information had been provided. Charley pushed for more. "You live here, right? I'm sorry, I don't know your name."

"Yes, I live here. The name's Toby, Toby Hooper."

"Do you like it here?"

"I love it here. It's the best place I've ever lived." A hint of a smile flashed across Toby's face.

The tour ended when Toby came to a stop on the second floor in front of a dirty brown wooden door. "This is the apartment that's for rent. I've never been in this one before."

Charley turned to Toby, forehead wrinkled, wondering just how many of these apartments Toby had wandered through. As he turned his head, he caught sight of an eviction notice posted on the door across the hall. "What's that about?"

"That's just Jimmie," Toby said with a slight grin. "He likes to joke around. He's really a great guy."

Toby inserted a key into the door and turned the tarnished brass doorknob. When he opened the door and glanced around the apartment, Toby's eyes lit up.

Walking across the creaky wooden floors, Charley watched Toby slowly come to life. As they stepped into the bathroom, Toby seemed in awe as he pointed to the tub. "Isn't that the most *lovely* antique claw-foot tub you've ever seen," he gushed. "It's just beautiful. Truly beautiful."

Toby's tour took about ten minutes, which was about nine minutes longer than Charley thought necessary. When he finished, Toby took one last look around, admiring every detail as if he were an archeologist who'd just discovered King Tut's tomb. "Wow! Whatchya think?"

"It's quaint," Charley said, being polite. "The rent, it's five hundred, right?"

"Yes," Toby said, mildly annoyed at the question. "It's lovely, don't you think?"

"It's good enough and the rent's right. I guess I'll take it. What do I have to do?"

Toby sensed Charley didn't share his passion for the apartment. "You'll have to go to the realty office." Irritation splashed across his face. "They'll want the first one and a half-month's rent. Then you'll get the key."

Belatedly, Charley realized his lack of enthusiasm for the apartment had wounded Toby and tried to heal him. "I'm really looking forward to moving in and being your neighbor".

"Yes." Toby spoke in a dull monotone. "I'll probably see you around."

Charley's right hand was left hanging. Feeling a bit guilty, he moved away, leaving Toby slumping by the door.

Toby, however, came back to life moments later as Charley walked down the stairs. "Oh, I almost forgot the best part of all." Toby was standing on tiptoes at the top of the stairs waving his arms with wild abandon. "You'll be right across from Jimmie. You'll like him. *Everybody* likes Jimmie."

Chapter 3
Paraphrasing

After shelling out seven hundred fifty bucks to the real estate agency, Charley had a little over a thousand and some change in his checking account. He had a studio apartment with no furniture, no job, and he owed the Chicago Police Department a hundred bucks.

Although he seemed to have every reason to be depressed, he felt strangely exhilarated as he walked to the Ginger Man tavern. He couldn't wait to give his good news to Lizzy.

When he sauntered into the bar, Lizzy was pouring a beer from one of the taps. Her eyes caught Charley the moment he opened the door and it seemed as if the temperature of her body elevated a degree or two at the sight of him. A white Cubs jersey hung over the waistline of his blue jeans. On his head was a blue baseball cap with a red "C" above the brim. There was a sweet innocence about him that caused those darned butterflies to stir in her stomach again. Stay cool, she reminded herself. Keep in control.

A whole day at the bar had given Lizzy a lot of time to analyze the previous night. Doing so convinced her to subdue her emotions.

Plopping down in the stool he'd sat on the night before, Charley smiled when he caught Lizzy's eye. In return, she offered an abrupt smile before returning her focus to the customer whose beer she'd just poured.

"That'll be four dollars," she said. The urge to turn her attention to Charley pressed hard on her heart.

The customer gave Lizzy a five-dollar bill and told her to keep the change. She thanked him, put the five in the cash-register drawer, removed a single and stuffed it in her black bra. For an instant, she gazed at the wall. Then she took a deep breath and turned to Charley.

"Hey, I thought I'd chased away all of you die-hards from this dump," she teased.

Charley was feeling warm, too. "Hi, Liz, it's good to see you, too."

"So, how'd it go today?"

"Well, I got an apartment." Charley paused to gauge Lizzy's response. On a scale from one to ten, his news seemed to have registered a zero. "That place on Bradley. We're only a couple of blocks from each other. I already started moving in."

The smile that had brightened Lizzy's face faded until eventually it disappeared, leaving a trail of questions behind.

"What?" Charley asked. The silence pained him. "Is that a problem?"

Lizzy knew she hadn't masked her disappointment well. She'd hoped–even prayed, something she rarely did–that Charley would change his mind. That he would come back to the bar and ask if he could stay with her. "Hey, that's ... that's great. I'm glad it worked out for you. It sounds ... it sounds great."

"But I haven't told you anything about it yet." Charley watched Lizzy's eyes wander as if they were searching for a hiding place.

"Oh. Yeah. I'm sorry, what did you say?" Her eyes shifted focus to a bar towel that she was flipping between her hands.

"Are you okay? You seem like you're a million miles away tonight."

"Oh, no. I mean yes. I'm fine. It's just been kind of busy around here today."

Charley glanced around the bar. A couple sat at one table in the corner. Besides Charley, the only other customer sitting at the bar was the man Lizzy had just served. Charley realized that he'd seen that same man the night before. He recognized him because, like the previous night, he was busily jotting into a notebook.

"I thought that maybe you'd like to come by my new apartment after work." Charley pressed on, hoping he could ignite the fire again. "It's not much. In fact, I don't even have any furniture yet. I do seem to have some interesting neighbors, though."

Lips parted but no words followed.

"Hey, I've got it. We can get a nice bottle of wine and some Chinese food and have a little picnic on the floor. It'll be fun. How 'bout it?"

Biting her lip, Lizzy restrained her desires. As much as she wanted to go wherever he might take her, she had to trust her instincts, which told her to back away. "I can't make it tonight," she finally blurted out.

"Why not?" Charley knew he had no right to ask that question, but he needed to know.

"I'm exhausted, Charley. I'm working a double-shift today. As you can see, I'm the only person in here today. My relief called in sick. By the time I get out of here it will be 1:30, and all I'll want to do is go to bed–something it doesn't sound like you have in your new apartment yet. Not that I think you're even interested in that aspect of a relationship."

The anxiety that had been building inside Charley now over-spilled like a dam that had burst. He hadn't seen the left hook coming. Now that it had struck, he knew that it was over. He turned serious with Lizzy, perhaps for the first time since they'd met. "We're friends, aren't we?"

"I … I don't know, Charley. You ask me if we're friends. How am I supposed to answer that? I met you in this bar, on that same stool, one night ago. I know nothing about you, other than that you're lost and trying to find yourself again. I get the feeling you want me to help you find your way. But I think that's something you're going to have to do on your own. When you do find your way, I hope you come looking for me again. I don't know if I'll still be here. I can't make that kind of promise, but I guess that's the chance you take when you don't take what's right in front of you."

After holding her emotions intact for longer than she could bear, it felt good for her to have let it all out. She was proud of herself for saying what she needed to say. Yet she also felt empty inside.

Charley's eyes sank into hers and he touched the skin of her left cheek with the fingertips of his right hand. The warmth of his fingertips spilled out as they made their way down the cheek until they fell off at the end of her face.

"You're something else," he said, "and I mean that in a good way–an unbelievably good way. You're right. I do need to get my shit together. That's basically what you're saying, isn't it?"

A warm but cautious smile arose on Lizzy's face. "I guess that's one way to paraphrase it. You're just a little more succinct than I am. Must be that journalistic training."

"I'm not going to say good-bye. That sounds too final. I don't want you to give up on me. I certainly don't plan to give up on you."

"Of course you won't give up on me. You're a die-hard."

Charley chuckled. Although it hurt him to let her go, he knew he had to do it. "I must be the dumbest man on this planet."

Lizzy bent over the bar and put her hands on Charley's shoulders, pulling his face into hers. "You're a Cubs fan. There's a lot more out there just as dumb as you are."

Putting both palms on his cheeks, she moved in and kissed him gently. As she did so, her knees trembled. "Just don't wait for the Cubs to win the World Series before you come looking for me."

Charley smiled, backed away and ambled toward the door. When he reached the door, he stopped, turned and looked once more at Lizzy. He painted her face in his mind, but left out one detail that his eyes weren't strong enough to see ... the tears that had welled in her eyes. With a tip of his cap he was then gone.

Chapter 4

First Impressions

Jimmie Dart hoped to make a good first impression on his new neighbor.

The polling results were in and they were all he needed–dark, handsome, and mysterious. Everything he wanted in a man.

Jimmie earned his living as a professional drag queen at The Baton on Clark. The pay was pretty good but the fringe benefits were better. He had the most delicious wardrobe imaginable. His tastes ran to the extravagant and changed with his mood. Today he felt like Marilyn Monroe–every man's wet dream.

So he slipped on a blonde wig, a brassiere with lots of lift and a hot red dress, then put on ruby-red lipstick and touched off his work by painting a mole on his left cheek and placing a white feather boa around his neck. The transformation was complete when he stepped into four-inch red high heels.

He checked himself out on the full-length mirror. "Girlfriend, you are H-O-T hot." Puffing out his lips, he blew a kiss at the mirror. "No man could resist this."

Like a model on the runway, he strutted out the door and across the hallway. At his neighbor's door, he lifted his left arm and clenched his fist. Sounds emanating from the apartment stopped him from knocking.

"Ooohhh! Mmmm! You feel soooo good inside me."

Intrigued, he decided to listen in a bit longer.

"Ooohhh! Ooohhh! Deeper. Deeper. There. That's it. Oh-oh-oh-ooooooohhhhh!"

Covering his mouth, he held back the laughter that was aching to spill out. He knew the sound of a porno flick when he heard it, and this was pure, 100 percent, unadulterated XXX stuff. "This is just too delicious," he cooed to himself.

What to do? His mind raced. Walk away? No way. This was too good of an opportunity to pass on. Besides, he'd gotten all dolled up. He didn't believe in getting all dressed up and having no place to go.

Instead, he put his right hand on the doorknob and gave it a slow turn. It was unlocked. He giggled, blunting the sound by covering his mouth. Now what? Knock or walk in? Reaching a compromise with his mischievous mind, he knocked twice and eased open the door without waiting for an invitation.

"Hold on." Charley scurried to find his boxers from underneath the sheets. "Just a second!" he cried, not noticing that his surprise guest had already let himself in.

"Hello neighbor." The ruby red lipstick dripped with moisture as he caught his first glimpse.

Startled, Charley sat upright in his futon, eyes and mouth frozen. He stared at … at … he wasn't even sure what it was.

"I hope I didn't catch you … at a bad time." Jimmie flipped his eyelids and smirked. Charley found himself paralyzed.

"I just wanted to introduce myself. I'm Jimmie. Jimmie Dart. We're neighbors. I live, well, I live right across the hallway from you."

Charley felt brain-dead. Although his heart beat rapidly, his mind seemed frozen.

The sounds of moaning and groaning emanating from his TV set shook Charley out of his stupor and he jumped for the remote. Pointing the remote at the TV, he fumbled for the power button. When he hit the target, the screen turned to snow. His arms remained outstretched as his hands clung to the remote.

Jimmie smirked again. "Maybe I've come at a bad time?" Charley nodded. Jimmie read the sign. "Don't be a stranger, handsome."

He cupped his right hand, put it to his mouth and blew a kiss to his handsome new neighbor. "Stop on by … *any* time you'd like. Like I said, I'm just across the hallway. You don't have to be scared of me. I don't bite. Okay. Sometimes. But not so it hurts."

Jimmie winked, turned and sashayed out the door.

Charley awoke the next morning thinking–hoping–it had all been a bad dream. As he got dressed, though, he noticed something on the floor that convinced him otherwise– a white feather.

He picked up the feather and held it in his palm, examining it with a curious mixture of fascination and disbelief. Then he put his lips together and blew. The feather rose up in a delicate glide and floated back down to the floor. The past was the past. The time had come to move on. There were more important things to worry about–mainly finding a job. His checking account was running on empty and rent was due in a couple of weeks. He didn't want to become the second tenant in the building to have an eviction notice posted on his door.

After debating with himself for several days over what to do with his life, he'd finally reached one conclusion. He needed to get back to reporting–the one thing he knew how to do and even enjoyed doing, at least most of the time. However, he knew it wouldn't be easy finding a job. The market for reporters was always tight–and even tighter for reporters with no experience. If he were to have any chance of getting a job, he couldn't bring up his history. That meant lying, something that didn't come naturally to him. He'd have to reinvent himself by erasing his past job as a reporter for the *San Francisco Star*. His own mind had already blotted out at least a portion of his life, something he didn't know how to account for, and certainly couldn't explain to a prospective employer.

For the past couple of weeks, he'd been picking up a copy of the *Northside Beat* at the convenience store around the corner, and he liked what he saw. The paper lacked the prestige of the city's two biggest papers, the *Herald* and the *Sun*, but it had a certain grittiness he found absent in many community papers. This just might be what he needed to get him back on his feet, and there just happened to be an opening for a fulltime courts reporter with a starting salary of three hundred fifty a week.

Managing to slip out of Bradley Place without bumping into his gender-twisting nightmare of a neighbor, he jumped into his car and chugged off in hopes of landing a job.

The office of the *Northside Beat* was in an old brick rehabbed warehouse, in the middle of a stretch of Lincoln Avenue dense with antique stores. Charley's heart pounded as he opened the heavy glass door to the building. Just getting to the point where he thought he could work again had been a major hurdle for him to clear. There were some memories that seemed to be lost for good. Others that he'd consciously locked away. Reporting would release some of the memories he didn't want to retrieve, but he had to start somewhere. He had to come to grips with what had happened and move on–and this was the time to do it.

Butterflies raced around in his stomach as he made his way to the reception desk and for a fleeting moment, he considered turning around. Instead he took a deep breath, settled his briefcase at his side and looked down at a bun of gray hair hanging over a crossword puzzle.

Lula Ann Preston Montgomery was a fixture of the *Beat*, as most people referred to the paper. A true southern belle who'd migrated north in the mid-fifties, she'd married once, to a much older, wealthy Chicago industrialist, Brandon Montgomery, who soon thereafter died, leaving her widowed, rich and bored. That was in 1960. Two years later, while reading the want ads in the *Beat,* she noticed an ad for a receptionist. She was hired on the spot. Although she never remarried, she was known to have had an affair with the paper's publisher, Jonathan Cooke, up until he passed away in 1990.

Now a spry seventy-eight-year-old, Lula Ann was the resident expert on the *Beat*'s storied eighty-year history, from the days when it was owned by Pulitzer to the day it almost went bust during the depression, only to be rescued by Cooke, then a young entrepreneur and aspiring newsman who had set out to turn Chicago and its infamous broad shoulders upside down. Though he didn't completely succeed, he'd somehow managed to keep the paper alive–though barely–for sixty years. When he died, he handed over command of what was then a sinking ship to his daughter, 32-year-old Dahlilah Cooke Edwards. This had the two big dailies licking their chops, thinking the paper would be sold. But Dahlilah, with no newspaper experience but an MBA from Stanford and a lot of gumption, elected to take on the big dailies. She instilled a David-versus-Goliath attitude and reversed the paper's conservative slant, making the paper more liberal both on its editorial pages and in how it was run. The changes caused many of the paper's old-time stable of readers to abandon ship. Only a handful of new readers jumped on board, leaving the paper right back where it started–drifting precariously toward financial ruin.

Lula Ann didn't at all like what Dahlilah had done. In Lula Ann's eyes, Dahlilah might as well have spat on her father's grave–and she was never one to shy away from her opinions. In fact, she let Dahlilah know what she thought just about every time she walked into the office. Many of the old staffers had come to believe she'd stayed on just to harass Dahlilah. The truth was she just didn't know what else to do with her life. Dahlilah was insightful enough to realize that, and she actually got a kick out of old Lula Ann, so she kept her on.

The problem was, Lula Ann wasn't a very good receptionist–never was. In most cases, she ignored people who approached the front desk–like now. Although she knew that Charley was trying to get her attention, she kept her head down and filled in squares in the crossword.

Eyes darting back and forth, Charley maintained a rigid posture as he tapped his fingers against his only suit. A few seconds passed before he cleared his throat. When that failed to attract Lula Ann's attention, he said, "*Excuse* me."

With a leisurely lift of her head, Lula Ann displayed the face that, thanks to plastic surgery, made her look a good twenty years younger than her true age. "May I *help* you?" A sweet touch of southern accent masked her generally sour demeanor.

"Um, yes." Charley's suit coat hid the perspiration stain on his white dress shirt.

"Well, *um*, maybe you could explain *how* I could help you." Lula Ann's eyelids flapped like a hummingbird's wings.

"Oh, yes, um, well, I'd like to see whomever's in charge of hiring for editorial staff."

"You mean Buzz?"

Charley lifted his brows. "If he hires the reporters, yes."

"I believe he does." Lula Ann knew full well that Buzz hired the reporters. She was the only *Beat* employee he hadn't hired–and that was because she was the only *Beat* employee who'd been there longer than he had. "He's the managing editor here."

"Well, then, do you think I could see him?" Charley adjusted his stance, so that he was standing in a rigid, military style.

"Let me see," she groaned. Turning away in a brusque manner, she picked up a telephone and punched a three-digit number. "Buzz, this is Lula Ann. There's a gentleman here at the front desk who'd like to speak to someone about a reporting job. I told him I thought he should probably talk to you." Her eyes moved down to the crossword puzzle and she filled in three squares before she said, "I'll send him back."

After putting down the receiver, she turned her attention to Charley. "You don't really want to work here, do you?" This was a test of the would-be reporter.

Charley squirmed. "Um, why, yes, I do."

"Well, I can't for the life of me know why anybody would want to work at a shit-hole like this, but if you insist, Buzz says he'll see you now."

Charley nodded, wondering whether he should be relieved or frightened. After picking up his briefcase, he began to amble past the receptionist desk until he realized he didn't know where he was headed. "Um, excuse me." Lula Ann smirked. "Excuse me, ma'am." Again, he was looking down at the bun of gray hair. "Can you tell me how to get to Buzz's office?"

Lula Ann unleashed a dramatic sigh. "Did you *say* something?"

For a moment, Charley thought he ought to consider another career, but then reminded himself that he didn't know how to do anything else. "I'm sorry, but I don't know where I'm supposed to go. Do you think you could point me in the right direction?"

Lula Ann worked up an insincere smile. "Well, of course, Blossom Buns. You'll find the old ogre all the way in the back. You can't miss him. He's got a protruding forehead and a massive overbite. Oh, and he's got the only office in the newsroom."

Charley offered a wary smile and scooted away. As he walked by a series of vacant 1950s-style desks, he wondered if the receptionist really had called him *Blossom Buns*. Next to the last desk, he found a door with a bronze plate on it spelling out in black lettering BUZZ BRADLEY.

Just as he was about to knock, the door swung open and an over-sized, hairy hand shot out. Charley grimaced as his right hand disappeared in the huge, bear-like paw.

"Saw ya coming through the glass. I'm Buzz Bradley. Everyone just calls me Buzz."

Charley raised his head in awe at the giant of a man, who had his shirtsleeves rolled up to expose the thick, dark, curly hair covering his skin. On his face, he wore a permanent five o'clock shadow.

Buzz instructed Charley to have a seat and motioned to one of two English oak conference chairs with upholstered arms and brass nail trim, which were situated at the edge of a large desk hidden under piles of newspapers. As Charley seated himself, Buzz settled into a tall-back, tufted, leather executive chair that had two chunks of black tape on the seat of it.

"So you're here about the reporter job?" Buzz hoped he'd found a suitable replacement for the former courts reporter, Tracy Bloggins, who had unexpectedly quit after six months and gone back to working as a salesclerk at Carson Pirie Scott, saying retail paid more, had better fringe benefits, less stress and more reasonable hours.

Charley said he was there for the job and pulled out his resume and the clips and citations from college, eight long years ago.

Buzz scanned the materials. The two shared the same alma mater and had gotten their apprenticeships at the *Illini Press.* That was all good, but reading Charley's account of the eight years since graduation caused Buzz to raise his dark, bushy unibrow. "So you've been working for Hunks-R-Us? That is a–"

"Exotic dance company," Charley said, finishing the sentence Buzz had been unable to complete. Telling Buzz the truth, that he'd been a copy editor and reporter at the *San Francisco Star* during those eight years, would have required him to answer questions he couldn't answer himself.

"Really?" Buzz lifted his brow as he awkwardly examined Charley's physique. "So you danced naked for money, for eight years?"

Charley gulped. The lie didn't seem to be holding up to scrutiny. "Yes, sir. It pays quite well."

"I'm sure. So why are you here then?"

"Well, to be quite frank, sir, the career of a male exotic dancer is a limited one. Although I'm only thirty-two, in the exotic dancing field, I'm considered a bit of a dinosaur. I knew I had to get out at some time and then I saw your ad for a reporter job in the paper. Well, I thought maybe I'd give it a shot."

Charley was surprised at how easily the lies came to him. The truth was he was almost enjoying himself.

Buzz shot a skeptical eye at Charley. The paper was missing out on some big stories by not having a fulltime courts reporter and couldn't afford to lose any more readers than it already had, but he couldn't be this desperate. Or could he? The job had been posted for two weeks and he'd received only a few inquiries about it and interviewed only two prospective reporters for the position. One didn't like the pay, and the other one was a hothead who'd been fired from a suburban weekly for making inappropriate comments at a village board meeting. Below the edge of the desk, Charley crossed his fingers.

Buzz pressed his hands to his temples, fighting back a headache. "I'll tell you what, Hubbs, I need a reporter, so I'm going to take a chance on you. I'll hire you on a trial basis. After one week, we'll decide whether you're cut out for this job or not."

Charley grinned. The ploy had worked. He had a job–or at least a trial job. Now he just had to prove himself worthy.

Buzz figured he'd be placing another ad in the paper for a courts reporter after the week was up. If he were in Vegas, he'd bet the would-be reporter would last no more than three days. So it was with a wary eye that he put out his gigantic paw. "You start first thing tomorrow."

"Thanks." The powerful clutch Buzz had on his hand caused him to wince. "I won't let you down."

"Yeah, well, we'll see about that."

One week later, Buzz withdrew a crisp twenty-dollar bill from his wallet and put it into the office charity jar. This was the first time he was happy to lose a bet with himself. Somehow, the stripper-turned-reporter had passed the test. Still, Buzz had doubts. Good fortune had a way of turning against him. The new reporter seemed too good to be true. There was no way he could do the job of the reporter, as he'd demonstrated, and have done it only in college before. So when Buzz told him that the job was his, he also whispered in his ear, "Don't make me regret this."

In the days that passed, Charley found that reporting slowly brought him back to life. The transition was difficult but not as tough as he thought it would be. The best part of the job was that it gave him something to think about other than his past. Soon, he was pumping out copy as good as anything in either of Chicago's two big dailies. This pleased Buzz and made Charley feel good for the first time in a long time.

Typing away at his computer until past deadline almost nightly, Charley often got lost in his work. That's what happened on Halloween night. After putting to bed a story on the arrest of an armed robber who'd terrorized banks on Chicago's North Side, he shut down his computer for the night a little after 9 P.M. He looked forward to just going home, crashing on his futon and sleeping through the weekend.

When he got back to his apartment around 10:15 P.M., he could tell that wasn't in the cards. Disco music blared from across the hall and costumed revelers knocked on Jimmie's door every five minutes or so. Charley imagined that Jimmie's studio apartment resembled a Volkswagen Beetle filled with clowns.

At 11 P.M., he laid down on his futon. The party noises permeating the thin walls, however, left him tossing and turning.

Around midnight, he rolled out of his futon and walked through the darkness to the kitchen. He opened the fridge and grabbed an Old Style, which he chugged down. The cold burn felt good in his throat and he popped a second, thinking cheap beer might be just the prescription for sleep. He downed the second almost as fast as the first, nearly coughing it up as he reached the bottom of the can. Then he grabbed a third can and carried it with him back to the futon. Propping himself against a pillow, he turned on the TV and surfed channels with one hand while sipping the Old Style that he clutched in the other. When he found one of his favorite horror classics, *Night of the Living Dead*, playing on AMC's weekend-long classic horror movie marathon, he set down the remote.

In the middle of the movie, he dozed off. His sleep didn't last long, however. At around 2:15, he was awakened by a knock at the door. On the TV, *The Creature from the Black Lagoon* had replaced the walking dead.

As he sat up and rubbed his eyes, there was a second knock on the door. Thinking it was likely an errant party-goer, or, worse yet, Jimmie himself, he ignored the knock. But then there was a third knock, this one slightly more forceful than the previous two, and there was a voice accompanying it–a *female* voice.

"Hello. Is there anybody in there? Hello. If you're in there, please open the door."

The soft, sexy voice intrigued Charley enough to get him out of bed. After stumbling across the dark room, he eased open the door, leaving the bolt lock attached. Through the crack between the door and wall, an eye caught his eye.

"Hi, I didn't wake you, did I?"

He glimpsed whiskers drawn onto the cheeks of a delicate face. "Oh, no, I was just lying in bed. I couldn't sleep."

"Oh. I just wanted to use your bathroom. There's a long line for Jimmie's and, well, I've *really* got to go."

"Oh. I suppose. I mean, yeah, sure."

When he unlatched the bolt lock, Charley opened the door to pointed black ears popping out of thin, strawberry-blond hair. Snug-fitting black leotards showed off a curvy body. After flicking the light switch by the door, he invited the comely kitten inside.

Sparkling green eyes made their way down to Charley's boxer shorts, decorated with hearts. The boxers had been a Valentine's Day gift from many years ago.

Realizing the attention his boxers had attracted, Charley blushed. "Sorry, I wasn't really expecting anyone."

"No reason to apologize," the mysterious feline purred. A tantalizing smile rose on her face as she waltzed by, trailing a long black tail.

Fortune had dropped itself at Charley's door in the form of a wayward sex kitten. Charley hurried to the closet, where he withdrew a pair of jeans and a *Fighting Illini* T-shirt out of the laundry basket. Just as he was tucking the T-shirt into his jeans, the door to the bathroom opened.

"You didn't have to get dressed on my account."

"I didn't really feel comfortable standing before a complete stranger in my boxers."

"We're not really complete strangers." She stared confidently into his eyes.

"But we've never met, at least as far as I know."

"You're right. We've never met, but that doesn't mean I don't already know a lot about you. I know you sleep in your boxers. I know you have trouble sleeping at night. I even know what cologne you use."

"I'm not wearing cologne."

"Polo by Ralph Lauren. I just saw the bottle on the sink."

"Okay, but you don't know my name."

"Sure I do. It's Charley."

Charley scratched his head. How did she know his name? Had she asked about him before coming over? Was there more to her visit than met the eye?

"Word gets around pretty fast at Bradley Place," she said.

What did she mean by *that*? Charley was finding his new home to hold more questions than it had answers. The reporter in him should have told him to investigate matters further, but his male instinct took over instead. Questions could be answered later. For now it was enough that she said her name was Leah Gandalet and that she lived in the apartment directly above him.

"It's nice to meet you, Leah. To be honest, it's a relief. I was afraid you were someone else."

She looked at him with whiskers bent. "Someone else?"

"It's just that the only other person to knock on that door since I moved in was a man dressed up to look like Marilyn Monroe."

Leah nodded knowingly. "That must be Jimmie. He's really a great guy--just a little eccentric. You just have to get to know him."

Charley recalled hearing similar praise for Jimmie from Toby. As far as he was concerned, the verdict on his cross-dressing neighbor was still very much out. For now, the beautiful stranger in a cat costume was the only neighbor he wanted to get to know better.

Lifting her head a bit, Leah batted her exaggerated cat-like lashes. "I just had a great idea. Why don't you come back to Jimmie's with me?"

"You're kidding, I hope." Charley laughed at the idea.

"No, really. It'd be fun."

Charley contemplated her offer a bit further. Although he had good reason to decline the invitation, he found himself unable to resist the charms of a frisky feline. "Okay," he relented. "I'll come over, but just for a little while."

"Great!" Leah kissed him on the right cheek, making him blush again. As she did this, she smiled slyly. *Mission accomplished*, she purred to herself.

Jimmie's apartment was a psychedelic funhouse. A disco ball hung in the middle of the main room. A strobe light flickered in the corner. Lava lamps glowed in various places. Elvis on black velvet hung on the wall.

The crowd fit the decor. As Leah dragged him through the room, Charley found himself doing double takes, unable to distinguish the costumed from the un-costumed–and with some, the male from the female.

Leah was oblivious to it all, fighting through the crowd with single-minded conviction. Her road led to a punch bowl shrouded in a dry ice fog. Once there, she reached for a plastic cup and spooned it full of a purple liquid. "Here, try this."

"What *is* this stuff?" Charley asked with curled lips.

"Jimmie calls it Purple Haze. It's good. Try it."

With an apprehensive eye, Charley raised the cup to his lips and took a timid sip. "Wow," he coughed. "This stuff packs quite a load. What's in it?"

"I don't know. We'll have to ask Jimmie." After pouring a cup for herself, she raised it for a toast. "To the beginning of a beautiful friendship."

"*Casablanca,*" Charley shot back.

Leah returned a puzzled look. "Huh?"

Charley chuckled. "I thought … you know, never mind. To us." Following Leah's lead, he raised his plastic cup and tapped it on hers.

After the toast, their eyes met for a split second. Leah wasn't ready to reel him in just yet, so she cast her eyes away. For now, she was playing the role of a demure kitten. Although the mousetrap was set, she was a cat that wanted to play with her intended prey for a while. Luring Jimmie into her game was like putting a nibble of cheese on the trap.

At first, Charley didn't hear Leah's suggestion that he be reintroduced to Jimmie. The party noises muted her gentle purr. When she repeated her overture with her lips to his left ear, Charley choked on the Purple Haze again. "I don't know if I'm ready for that. I might need a few more glasses of this stuff."

On cue, Charley's empty cup was swiped from him.

"Here, let me service you," Jimmie said with a wide grin.

Out of costume, Charley didn't recognize his neighbor. Jimmie, with his dyed-blond, short-cropped hair, black turtleneck and skin-tight blue jeans, was a stylish, almost debonair man.

After pouring a cup full of Purple Haze, Jimmie topped it off with a spray of whip cream from a can. "I like my liquid topped with cream," he said with a shrug of his shoulders and a slight smile as he handed the cup back to Charley.

"Thanks," Charley said. "I don't think we've met."

"Oh, but we have," Jimmie shot back confidently. "We certainly have."

Charley examined the man standing before him–his muscular six-foot frame, chiseled jaws, slightly pointed nose and haunting hazel eyes didn't provide a clue. "I'm sorry. You don't look familiar to me."

Jimmie smirked, enjoying the game he was playing. "Well, you only saw me in my, uh, professional attire."

Still Charley didn't see it. "Maybe you could refresh my memory. I'm usually pretty good at remembering a face."

Jimmie offered an almost sadistic smile this time. "Maybe if I told you my profession, it would help you. I work at The Baton. You've heard of The Baton, haven't you?"

Charley still looked puzzled. "I don't think so. Should I have heard of it?"

Tired of watching Jimmie's game and having the attention stolen from her, Leah broke in. "Charley, meet Jimmie Dart."

Jimmie's grin widened as he watched Charley freeze. "Oh," he chirped, "now you remember."

Charley gulped down the cup of Purple Haze, but it failed to loosen him up.

Again, Jimmie came to his rescue by heisting the cup from him and refilling it with Purple Haze. "I owe you an apology. I was a very, very bad boy when I…" Jimmie mocked clearing his throat. "Well, when I walked in on you a while back."

With another gulp, Charley's cup was empty once again. His head felt empty, too. Worse yet, it was spinning like a Tilt-A-Whirl.

"You're a quiet one, aren't you?" Jimmie was growing bored.

Leah's eyes darted between the two. "Are you all right, Charley?"

"I'm just feeling a bit light–" As his words faded, his skin tone turned pale.

"That Purple Haze can carry a wallop," Jimmie said with temperate concern. Having hosted many a party, Jimmie was accustomed to a few dropouts.

Charley's world now turned blurry. With all the strength he could muster, he said, "Maybe I should go back to my apartment."

Leah now took control. After seizing Charley's empty cup, she set it on the table and turned to Jimmie. "I'm going to help him back to his apartment."

"Sure," Jimmie said with a wink. "It was so nice meeting you, Charley. We'll have to have a little heart-to-heart when you're a little bit more, uh, lucid."

With his head bobbling, Charley held onto Leah's right hand as she guided him through the crowd, out the door, into his apartment, and onto his futon.

As Leah comforted him on her lap, Charley gazed up at her through blurred eyes. "Thank you for rescuing me. You've been very kind. I don't know what came over me."

"I think you just drank the Purple Haze a little too fast. You'll be okay. You're looking better already."

Charley nodded as Leah took her right hand and brushed her fingers through his wavy hair. Her hand made its way to his face and her soft skin felt good on his unshaven cheeks. As she slid her index finger around his lips in a delicate dance, her own lips inched closer to him. Charley gulped.

Like a cat on the prowl, Leah now moved in for the kill. Putting her lips to his, she pushed against him with her chest, easing him down on the futon.

Charley's mind had gone numb. His body was warm and damp with sweat, and it felt like he'd escaped his body and was floating on a cloud. This was heaven.

But this heaven opened up into hell. The cloud burst and he fell through, plunging head first, like a missile.

Faster. Faster. Faster. He was on a runaway elevator. Faster. Faster. Faster.

"Stop! Stop! Stop!" he cried. But he couldn't stop himself. This time he was going to crash.

Persistent knocking on the door jolted Charley out of his terrifying free fall. Soaked in sweat, shaking, and naked, he tried to get his bearings. Then he remembered–Leah. Where was she?

"Charley, are you okay? It's Jimmie. Open up."

Jimmie? Why was he knocking on the door at this time of day? He glanced at his alarm clock. It read 5:15 P.M. What happened to the morning, he wondered.

"Charley, are you all right in there? Come on. Open the fucking door!"

Confused, Charley yelled out, "Wait!" A sharp pain shot through his head, like an electrical shock. "Hold on–just a second."

As he tried to stand, his legs trembled and he reached for the wall for support. After balancing himself, he stumbled to the closet, where he grabbed a towel and put it to his face and ran it down his soaking chest and legs. Once he was dried, he threw on the musty-smelling T-shirt and jeans he'd worn the night before.

There were more knocks on the door and Charley cried out, "I'm coming!" Again, he felt a sharp pain in his head.

Opening the door a crack, Charley glimpsed the concerned expression on Jimmie's face. "What's the matter with you?"

Jimmie pushed the door open and stormed inside. "I was going to ask the same question of you. You were screaming like a fucking maniac. I thought you were in trouble or something … boy, you look like hell."

Charley scratched his head. "Really?"

"Yeah. Really. I heard you from across the hallway. You were screaming and then you started yelling 'Stop! Stop! Stop!' I didn't know what the hell to think. Quite frankly, you were scaring the livin' shit outta me, and the way you looked when you left the party last night, well…"

"Huh," Charley said, scratching his head. "I must have had some kind of a nightmare or something. I must admit I have only vague memories of last night. Do you know what happened to Leah?"

"Leah?" Jimmie looked quizzically at Charley. "Leah–the girl who dragged me over to your party last night."

"Oh, Catwoman. Sorry, I didn't know her name–interesting name. So did you get Leah'd last night, Charley boy? Ha-ha-ha! Oh, I crack myself up sometimes."

Charley stared blankly at Jimmie, too weary and in too much pain to tolerate jokes.

Realizing he was laughing alone, Jimmie cut himself off. "Boy, are we a fuddy-duddy, or what? So … where were we? Oh, yes, Catwoman. I wouldn't know where she is. She's a friend of yours, is she?"

"No, I just met her last night." Charley slowed his speech a notch to avoid intensifying the throbbing pain in his head. "I thought she was a friend of yours."

Jimmie flipped his palms. "No. Maybe. I don't know. How do you really know who your friends are? Are we friends?"

"I'm really confused now."

"You? And I thought I was the one who was confused."

"But Leah … I don't know … it just seemed like … well, she acted like she knew you really well." Charley's head felt like a wrecking ball was crashing into it.

"Sorry, Charley. Nobody knows me really well. The fact is I just met her at the party last night, just like you."

"Huh?" Charley shook his head, thinking he might have misheard or misunderstood what Jimmie had just said.

"You've got quite a vocabulary, Charley. Well, really, I just wanted to make sure you were okay."

"Yeah, I'm okay. Hey…"

"Yes?"

"Thanks."

"Not at all. You'd have done the same for me, right?"

"I'm not so sure." Charley smiled, and then put a hand to his temple as he felt another throb of pain.

"You would," Jimmie said. "I can tell."

Chapter 5
The Kicker

On the Monday following his lost weekend, Charley arrived at work at 9 A.M., three hours early. He liked to get a jumpstart on the competition. On days when he had to be in court, he started as early as seven. He was relieved this wasn't one of those days. Feeling like his body had served as a punching bag all weekend, he didn't think he would have been able to get out of bed any earlier than he had, and he wasn't at all ready for the insanity of court. No, a nice restful day sitting at his cozy desk was just what the doctor ordered.

Although he had a lot of calls to make, he put them off, grabbed the weekend papers and tried to catch up on the news.

On his desk, he laid out Saturday's *Beat*. The story he'd written about the arrest of the armed robbers made the front page, below the fold. Seeing that he'd made Page 1 lifted his spirits, but the good feeling was a fleeting one. Reading over the story, he scowled at the hack copy-editing job that had marred his once-clean prose. "Two Chicago men were charged with the armed robbery" had been altered to read, "Two Chicago men were charged with the *alleged* armed robbery"–as if the armed robbery might not have occurred. Having begun his career as a copy editor himself, Charley knew that copy editors worked dreadful hours, under demanding deadlines, so he was able to forgive many, if not most of their sins–but the one sin he couldn't excuse was misusage of the word alleged. He'd gone through many a bottle of Pepto-Bismol over that one maddening word.

So it was with a sigh that he folded up the Saturday paper and then skimmed through Sunday's and opened Monday's–his usual Monday morning routine. Reading through Monday's paper, he found his eyes drawn to a four-paragraph brief in the local crime section with the headline WOMAN'S BODY FOUND IN LAKEVIEW DUMPSTER. The story described an elderly resident's discovery of an unidentified woman's naked body in a trash dumpster in an alleyway next to where Charley lived. The body had been found Sunday morning. The story said police reported no information as to the cause of death and that an autopsy was to be performed, but what caught Charley's eye was the description of the woman as being in her early twenties with strawberry-blond hair.

Three times he read the brief, and with each reading a chill ran down his spine. The description of the dead girl seemed to jump out at him like a ghost from a closet.

A slap on his back shook him out of his stupor.

"How's it going, Charley?" Charley recognized Buzz's gruff voice. His early-morning prayer that Buzz would leave him alone, at least until he could recover from his weekend hangover, had not been answered.

Turning to face his editor, Charley put on his best poker face and lied, claiming he was fine.

"You don't look so fine," Buzz said, concerned. "You look like you saw a ghost."

"No, really, I'm fine. I just didn't sleep very well last night."

Buzz nodded. "Liked your story on the armed robber. It's about time they caught that scoundrel."

His mind elsewhere, Charley didn't hear his editor's words. Without acknowledging the compliment that had been paid him, he jumped into the question that was troubling him. "Say, you wouldn't happen to know who wrote this story, would you?"

Buzz scratched his furry head. "Gee, I can't be sure, since I wasn't here over the weekend, but I'd guess Piper. He does most of the crime beat stuff for us."

Piper was Danny Piper, a hard-drinking Irish curmudgeon whose tenure with the *Beat* was longer than that of any other reporter.

"Why, might I ask?" Buzz asked. "You got something?"

Knowing Buzz was always fishing for a story, and concerned that he might be subjected to questions he didn't want to face, Charley dropped the issue. "No reason. Just curious."

Piper didn't work Mondays. The weekend crime beat kept him too busy. That made Monday recovery day, and he didn't like to be disturbed on recovery day.

Charley had heard stories of the now-legendary Irish fits Piper threw when he got a call from work on his day off. Nobody made that mistake twice. So it was with a great deal of trepidation that Charley, on lunch break, picked up the phone. He needed to know what Piper knew, if anything, and he couldn't wait another day to find out.

On the second ring, Piper, half-asleep, picked up the phone, offering only silence to his caller. Riley, a golden Labrador, watched him from his place at the end of the bed.

"Hello? Piper, is that you?" Perspiration began collecting around Charley's collar. "It's Charley. Charley Hubbs–from the paper."

Though he'd been working at the *Beat* for a few weeks, Charley had spoken only once with Piper–and that could hardly be taken as a conversation. A couple days after being hired fulltime, Charley approached Piper at his desk and introduced himself, thinking it was the professional, polite, friendly thing to do. Piper glanced up from a newspaper he was reading, nodded, grunted, and returned his eyes to the paper. That was his *relationship* with Piper. He couldn't be sure if Piper even knew who he was, but Piper quickly vanquished that doubt.

"Sorry, kid, I thought you were that friggin' editor."

Although Piper seemed cordial enough, Charley was uncomfortable about calling him. He had no right digging into a story that wasn't his, and Piper had every right to brush him aside. Still, the description of that girl ... he couldn't shake it. No, he had to forge on. Piper had a weakness, and right now, Charley wasn't above exploiting it to his advantage. "Say, there's something I'd like to talk to you about," Charley said. "You've been around the *Beat* a long time. You can probably fill me in on some of the people here. What say we meet at Sheffield's this evening for a beer? I'll buy."

I'll buy. That's all Piper needed to hear. He never met a beer he didn't like, and he never turned one down. "I'll meet you there about seven."

A few short weeks ago, Sheffield's beer garden was abloom in a colorful array of khaki shorts and bright-colored skirts. Now, there were only barren picnic tables and dead leaves scattered on the ground. Inside, a lonely log burned in the fireplace, a reminder that Chicago's unforgiving winter would soon come calling.

On this Monday night, the bar was almost empty. A rowdy group of guys wearing college sweatshirts hunched around a big-screen TV watching Monday Night Football while building an impressive tower of Hamm's beer cans. A slate chalkboard above the bar announced that Hamm's was the special "Bad Beer of the Month."

Charley sat alone at the bar tapping his fingers on a pint of Honker's Wintertime Ale. Almost two months had now gone by since he'd said good-bye to Lizzy. *My, how time flies, even when you're not having fun.* Dismayed, he shook his head, put the glass to his lips and tilted his head back. This wouldn't wash away his sorrows, but it would ease the pain a bit.

As he came through the front door, Piper eyed Charley downing the beer and smirked. He'd been there–many times. On Charley's back, he rested a venous, red-freckled hand. "Hey, kid, save some for me." A knowing wink followed.

Piper was wrapped in a gray, weathered trench coat. He also wore some of the physical signs of alcoholism–tremulous hands, red eyes, puffy face.

Charley's father had worn those same features, and had died of alcoholic cirrhosis at 59. Was Charley getting a glimpse of what the future held for him?

"What can I get you?" Charley asked, shaking off his concerns as he always did.

Piper ordered a Guinness, and Charley ordered a second beer for himself. A little boldness booster was in order.

Piper didn't need a shot of courage. Tenaciousness was natural for him. He jumped right on Charley.

"Thanks for the beer, kid," Buzz said. "Now, tell me, what's *really* up?"

"What do you mean?" Charley had been broadsided.

"You know. Callin' me at home on my day off. Somethin's gotta be up. I know ya didn't just call me out here to talk office politics."

The gig was up. Charley knew it and admitted his sin. He'd lied to get

Piper to answer questions about the murdered girl, but he didn't tell Piper why he wanted to know–and that left him vulnerable.

"You know somethin'" Piper said, "maybe you killed her. Is that what this is kid, a confession?" Piper poked Charley with his index finger. "Now that would be a story." Charley remained stone-faced. Piper's grin widened and he gave Charley a forceful nudge just below the right shoulder. "Hey, chill out, kid. I'm just yankin' yer chain."

Charley breathed a momentary sigh of relief. Beads of sweat had started to form on his forehead and around his collar. After gulping down some beer and clearing his throat, he launched into his investigation. There were many questions he had, but he didn't want to tip off Piper as to his reason for wanting to know. Pressing him too hard would make him suspicious. No, he had to remain cool, calm and collected. When the time came, he'd show his cards–but not yet. Information was valuable, and Piper had it. Charley just had to coax it out of him. Patience was in order. A couple more beers and it would come.

As it turned out, Piper's lips loosened like a sieve by the fourth Guinness. He spilled everything he had. "The body hasn't been officially identified, 'ya know," Piper said, "but off-the-record, between yuze and me, I heard she was a high-priced call girl–a very hot one. She went by the name of Leah Gandalet."

At the mention of the name, Charley choked on his beer and his face turned pale.

"You okay, kid? You look like you saw a ghost."

Charley gulped down the rest of his beer. "Yeah, I'm fine. I think I need another beer. What about you?"

Piper nodded. "Hey, you're all right, kid."

Charley smiled and threw another ten at the bartender and held up two fingers. His mind raced. He tried to put all the pieces of the puzzle together, but there were too many missing pieces. Leah had to have been killed sometime between the time he blacked out Saturday morning and the time she was found Sunday morning. That put him square in the middle of this mess.

Charley hoped his reaction to the mention of Leah's name hadn't blown his cover. Now he really had a lot of questions. Would Piper still be a willing informant? Two beers later he got the extra information he needed. The cops didn't know the cause of death and an autopsy was scheduled for the next morning. Charley needed more.

"But they do believe she was murdered, right?" Charley prodded.

"Well, somebody put her in that dumpster. I don't think she climbed in there herself," Piper guffawed.

"Yeah, I guess you're right." Charley offered an uneasy smile and pressed on. "Is there a suspect?"

"They've got nothin', kid—not a clue. They're hopin' somebody saw somethin'. Obviously, somebody put her in that dumpster. They think maybe somebody saw her get dumped. So far, though, they don't got any leads."

Charley nodded and then gulped down the rest of his beer. He slid his glass to the edge of the bar and motioned for the bartender.

"Another?" Charley asked Piper.

Piper responded by putting his glass to his mouth, jerking his head back and letting the beer flow down his throat in a single, swift motion. When the glass was empty, he slammed it down on the bar, slid it to the edge next to Charley's. "Keep 'em comin', kid."

At 1:30 A.M. on a Tuesday, Bradley Place was a dark forest. Monday was a night off for the party crowd. The only other time it was ever this quiet there was in the afternoons, before the next night of partying started.

In a drunken stupor, Charley, fumbling with his keys outside the door to his apartment, turned to look across the hallway. Emboldened by the beer, he took a deep breath and turned around. At Jimmie's door, he gulped, lifted his arm and readied his fist to knock. Inches from the door, he called back his fist.

For a moment, he stood there in an awkward pose, his beer-fogged brain stuck in the mud. When he managed to free himself, he lurched toward Jimmie's door with fist clenched. There, he'd done it. Now, he just had to face him. He paced back and forth as his eyes kept making their way toward Jimmie's door. A few seconds passed without an answer, so he turned back to the safety of his own apartment. Sleep it off and in the morning he'd be able to make a clear-headed decision on whether to try again. As he was inserting the key into his door lock and thanking his lucky stars that Jimmie wasn't home, Charley heard a door squeak from behind.

With a sigh, he turned to face Jimmie. Instead of Jimmie there was a thinly built man with olive-brown skin and greasy dark hair, messed from sleep.

"Did you knock?" the man at the door asked, each word spoken with slow precision in a smooth Polynesian accent.

"Uh ... yeah." Confusion wore on Charley's face like a tailored suit. "You're not Jimmie."

"No," the stranger said with a yawn. "Jimmie's working tonight. I don't expect him back for at least a couple hours."

"Oh. I'm sorry to have bothered you."

"Hey, it's all right. I pretty much expect it when I stay at Jimmie's. I don't think we've met. I'm Elvis. Elvis Pilapapaya."

"Hi, uh ... Elvis?" Charley thought of the picture of *the* Elvis hanging in Jimmie's apartment. "Sorry, but you don't look like an Elvis."

Elvis launched into a well-rehearsed explanation of the origin of his name. He said he was from Samoa, an island in the South Pacific, and that his parents were both huge fans of Elvis Presley. In honor of the king of rock 'n' roll, they named their first-born son after him. "Quite a cruel little joke to play on a kid, don't you think?"

There were many questions that Charley could have asked, but instead he just smiled and said, "My name's Charley. I live across the hall."

Elvis had already gotten the heads up on his handsome neighbor. "Yes, I've heard quite a bit about you. Nice to meet you, Charley. I'll be sure to tell Jimmie you stopped by."

Charley wasn't sure what to make of Elvis' comment, but he'd come to accept that Bradley Place Apartments was full of odd characters and a few mysteries. In the morning, he'd be ready to explore those further. Right now, he just wanted to dive into his futon and forget for a while.

Charley awoke to the buzz of his alarm clock at seven the next morning. Battling the punishing effects of a hangover, he managed to shower, dress himself and make it to the office by 8 A.M. At that hour, the office was empty except for the circulation department, which consisted of a married couple, Bob and Arlene Kraczinski, who spent much of their time at work arguing.

On his way to work, Charley had struggled to recall pieces of his night with Leah Gandalet, but they weren't falling into place. After scanning the paper to make sure there were no more surprises, he broke newsroom protocol and dialed the Medical Examiner's office to ask about the status of the autopsy. This was Piper's story, and he had no right delving into it. As it turned out, he didn't get anywhere anyway. He got an answering machine from the desk of the public information officer and hung up without leaving a message.

The rest of the morning he frittered away. There were calls to make that he put off. Mail, piled high on his desk, went untouched. There were follow-up stories to be written that he let die. All of this went against his character. After wasting three hours, he got up from his desk and, without telling Buzz or anyone else, left work and headed back to Bradley Place. Something was nagging at him that could only be scratched there.

When he entered the building, he went straight to the mailboxes. He wasn't checking mail. He was checking names. As he figured, not one mailbox had the name Gandalet on it.

Leah had told him that she lived in the apartment directly above his, so he made his way to the third floor. When he came to the apartment that matched his except for the first number being a three instead of a two he knocked and held his breath.

Toby Hooper opened the door–and another mystery for Charley. Two months ago, it was Toby who'd shown Charley the apartment. Now he looked at Charley as if he'd never seen him before.

"You don't remember me, do you?" Charley asked.

Toby tilted his head and examined Charley for a moment. No response followed.

"I'm Charley ... Charley Hubbs. You showed me the apartment, the one directly below here, about two months ago."

The tripwire to Toby's brain went off. "Yes. Now I remember. You're the guy across from Jimmie."

Charley had broken through. Now he needed to reach the next level. This wasn't easy. Toby had questions he wanted answered first. He wanted – *needed* – to know what Charley thought of the apartment.

Aching to move on to his own questions, Charley repeatedly assured Toby that the apartment was fine. This didn't calm Toby, however, so

Charley appeased him by explaining in vivid detail *everything* he liked about the apartment, even describing the joys of bathing in the claw foot bathtub. This relaxed Toby and allowed Charley to move on to the question of Leah Gandalet.

Toby claimed to have never heard the name Leah Gandalet, and Charley believed him. The more questions Charley asked, the more curious things became. Toby told him that he'd been in that same apartment for two years and that he'd lived alone the entire time. This didn't surprise Charley. Who'd live with a guy like Toby? Toby also denied knowing of anyone in the building who fit the description of Leah Gandalet. This was important. To get an apartment in the building, a prospective tenant would have gone through Toby first.

There was only one unmistakable conclusion to be reached. Leah had lied. The next obvious question was: *Why?*

Charley was back at work at a little after two in the afternoon. A small pile of messages had collected on his desk. One from Piper caught his attention and caused him to pick up the phone.

Piper answered on the first ring, as if he'd been expecting the call. "Yeah … hey, kid, I just got back from the M.E.'s office. Thought you'd be interested in what they had to say."

Charley swallowed the saliva that had built at the back of his mouth. Trying to sound cool and collect, he said, "Yeah. What you got?"

"Well, the official cause of death is a drug overdose … say, have you heard of the rave drug, ecstacy?"

"Yeah. I've *heard* of it." Stories had been popping up in the news recently telling how ecstacy had been gaining popularity at a number of clubs and *rave* parties where industrial or techno music is played loudly. People who use it, mostly teens and young adults, claim that it creates an almost peaceful feeling and amplifies physical sensations, including sexual ones.

"Well, that's what this girl probably thought she was takin'. In actuality, it looks like she was a victim of a more powerful and dangerous form of the drug. Ecstacy, or MDMA as it's also known, is rarely fatal. But what they found in her was a copycat drug known as PMA, or para … let me say this to you slowly, para-meth-oxy-amphetamine. Now, PMA hasn't been known to circulate here in the states much. But it's been around for a while in other countries. In fact, it claimed nine lives up in Canada in 1973 and at least six more died when the drug resurfaced in Australia recently. So it can be pretty potent stuff. The way it was explained to me, this PMA is more powerful than ecstacy. It doesn't take effect as quickly, though, so it encourages users to overdose."

Piper paused to gather his own thoughts and to let what he'd told Charley sink in. "You stayin' with me, kid?"

"Yeah." Perspiration beaded on his forehead. "Go on."

"When PMA does kick in, it can raise body temperature up to a hundred six degrees in people who overdose. In other words, this girl in the dumpster, she literally cooked from the inside out." Charley felt like he was cooking from the inside himself. "You still there, kid?"

"Yeah. Anything else?" Charley had already heard more than he wanted to hear, but he had a sickening feeling that there was more–and he was right.

"Well, yeah. Like I said, this girl probably thought she was taking ecstacy. The pills for PMA are typically sold to look exactly like ecstacy. That means this girl probably took these pills voluntarily. Obviously, though, it looks like somebody gave her the pills with the idea of killing her. Otherwise, how do you explain her naked body ending up in the dumpster, unless, of course, somebody just got scared and dumped her there? The cops really can't say for sure one way or the other at this point. So it's not officially being called a homicide. At least not yet."

"But they're leaning in that direction?" Charley chimed in.

"Homicide? Yeah, it seems so, kid."

"Thanks, Piper."

"Hey, no problem, kid. One last thing, though. There's a kicker to this one. They found semen in the girl. They say it looks like she had sex less than twenty-four hours before she died. My guess is you find the guy who boffed her and you find the guy who gave her the drug. But it doesn't sound like they have any leads yet. I'll keep you posted if I hear anything, though."

Silence followed Piper's words. Charley's heart felt like it had stopped. He didn't remember having sex with Leah, but, then, he didn't remember *not* having sex with her.

"You still there, kid?"

Piper's last question was left hanging because Charley had dropped the phone. The troubles that had plagued him once before–the same ones he thought he'd left behind–had come back for him. Of that Charley was now certain. He felt it in his bones. That God-awful cold chill had returned.

Chapter 6
Straight Talk

As Charley plodded to the office bathroom, the eyes gazing at him from the desks looked like a swarm of attacking bees. When he reached the bathroom, he secured the door behind him, but as he lifted the toilet seat, knelt and stared into the bowl, the bees came up through the plumbing and out of the pool at the bottom of the bowl and surrounded his face. The enemy army was about to fire. He closed his eyes. The sickness that had been churning inside of him was unleashed like a tornado.

Charley flushed the toilet. If only all of his troubles could be washed away with the flick of a handle. After rinsing his hands and splashing his face with cold water, he opened the door to another nightmare–his editor.

"Hey Charley, you okay?" Buzz asked out of sincere concern.

"Yeah … *yeah* … I'm fine," Charley replied, not so convincingly.

"You didn't look so fine when you went into that bathroom. You looked positively green."

Charley hated lying. Yet his whole relationship with Buzz had been built on a lie. Truth be told, he wouldn't have a job if he hadn't lied to get it. Now he was learning that a little lie is planted like a seed and just keeps growing, until the day it becomes too unmanageable and has to be chopped down. Someday he hoped to be able to tell the truth to Buzz, but this just wasn't that time.

"I think I got a touch of the flu. I feel better now, though."

Buzz knew a sick dog when he saw one. This one he sent home. "Get some rest. You can start fresh tomorrow."

Charley crashed on his futon in the afternoon. When he awoke, it was the dead of night–the time when Jimmie prowled. Charley's job was to find him and that meant operating on his clock.

Arising from the comforts of his futon, Charley tamed a severe case of bed head by slapping on a Cubs cap. The wrinkles in the red-striped Oxford shirt and khaki pants he'd worn to work earlier in the day he'd have to live with for now. There was work to be done and no more time to be wasted.

The first stop was across the hallway. Charley was pretty sure Jimmie would be out for the night, but he hoped Elvis would be home and that he'd be able to steer him in the right direction. When Elvis did answer the door, a silly thought struck Charley. Elvis *always* seemed to be in the building.

The news Elvis shared was good and bad. He knew where Jimmie could be found. The place where he could be found was the troublesome part for Charley. Jimmie was trolling at The Manhole, a gay bar located in the middle of a mile-long strip of Halsted known as Boys Town.

"It's Ladies Night," Elvis explained. "Ladies get drinks at half price. It should be fun. You might have a hard time finding Jimmie, though."

"Why's that?"

"Well, he's in drag, of course. Why do you think he's there? Half-price drinks."

Charley thought he now understood, but sought clarification. "So Ladies Night is just guys?"

"Well, yes, of course," Elvis said with a flip of his palms. "What other kind of ladies do you find in Boys Town?"

Elvis read Charley's distress signals and threw out a life preserver. "I need to get out of this apartment. I'll join you. Come on … it'll be fun," he said with a playful tap on the shoulder.

Charley bit his upper lip and, against his better instincts, relented.

"Good," Elvis chirped. "It's a date."

Pacing outside the blacked-out windows of The Manhole, Charley was having second thoughts. Elvis had spiked his hair and changed into tight black leather. Scanning the line outside, Charley observed that Elvis' attire was on the tame side.

"I don't think I can do this," Charley confided.

"Sure you can." For reassurance, Elvis wrapped his right arm around Charley's shoulders. "Just stay close to me." With a shake of his hips and a wink, Elvis removed his arm from Charley and pulled a compact mirror out of his pants pocket so that he could primp one last time.

As they inched closer to the bar, Charley grew more wary. "I *really* don't think I can do this."

Elvis had heard enough. "What's the problem, Charley?"

"This is a *gay* bar."

"Yes. It's a *gay* bar. Sooo…"

"I'm not gay."

With his mouth agape, Elvis placed his hands on his waist and scrutinized Charley. "My lord, I knew there was something wrong with you."

"I'm not kidding."

"Oh, Charley, I knew you were straight all along. We can tell, you know."

Charley had an admission. "The thing is I've never been in a gay bar. I don't know how to act."

Elvis shook his head in disbelief. Straight men were an enigma to him. How could you set a straight man straight? His answer was a simple one. "Just be yourself, Charley. Don't try to be someone you're not. Then you'd really stick out like a sore thumb. Listen, just stick with me. You'll be fine. I promise you won't come out of here any less straight than you already are."

Charley sighed, realizing, against all probabilities, that Elvis was making more sense than he.

The Manhole was dimly lit and, true to its name, decorated like a Chicago sewer system. After waiting in line to get into the bar, a second line awaited Elvis and Charley for the back bar and dance floor.

Judging by what he'd seen in the entry bar, Charley was feeling better about things. As they waited in the line for the back bar, he leaned into Elvis and said, "This isn't so bad."

Elvis returned a self-satisfied smile. "I told you it'd be okay."

A beefy, leather-clad bouncer stood between Charley and the door to the back bar. On the wall was a sign that read SHIRTS. NO SERVICE. Charley paid the sign no heed and went straight for his wallet. "What's the cover?"

The bouncer returned a blank stare and motioned to the sign on the wall.

Confused, Charley shrugged his shoulders and turned to Elvis for guidance.

At first, Elvis feigned ignorance, but he wasn't a good actor, and Charley saw right through him.

"Okay, what's goin' on, Elvis?"

Elvis had neglected to mention one small detail. On Ladies Night, it was bar policy that customers had to either be in drag or shirtless. That meant Charley was overdressed.

Charley turned grim. "You're telling me that if I want to find Jimmie, I'm going to have to take my shirt off?"

Elvis returned a crooked smile. "That's about it."

Charley shot a glare Elvis' way before returning his attention to the bouncer. "I have to take my shirt off to get back there?"

"That's the bar rule."

With a sigh and a shake of his head, Charley shed his wrinkled shirt and his pride.

The back bar and its environs was reminiscent of the bar scene in *Star Wars*–the queer, the peculiar and the bizarre ruling the stage. Hard-core gay porn was showing on a big-screen TV.

Charley felt as if he was in the junior high shower for the first time.

Reading Charley's discontent, Elvis tried to comfort him. "What's the matter?"

"I feel naked."

"What ... the shirtless thing? What's the big deal? I'm sure you wear less than that on the beach."

"This isn't the beach."

"Life's a beach." Elvis roared at his own joke but cut off his laugh when he realized that Charley wasn't laughing with him. "Charley, just loosen up. Have some fun. One day you'll be able to look back at this and laugh about it."

"Well, that day isn't today. Let's just find Jimmie and get the hell out of here."

"Okay-okay. Just hold your horses. We'll find him. That I promise you."

On the dance floor, Sylvester's "You make me feel (mighty real)" was booming out of large speakers at each corner. Charley trailed Elvis as they wormed and bumped their way into the middle of the dance floor. A thick fog smelling of burnt chocolate crept up around their feet. When Elvis put on the brakes, Charley's bare chest collided into Elvis' bare back. Elvis turned and apologized, a teasing smile on his face.

They trudged on until Elvis reported a sighting of a fruit hat dancing over the crowd. "That's Jimmie. Come on."

When he got an eyeful of Jimmie, Charley couldn't help but grin. Wearing a brightly flowered two-piece outfit with a bare midriff, topped off by the fruit headpiece, Jimmie was trying to mambo to the disco music.

Jimmie's frantic contortions came to a halt when he spotted Elvis. "What are you doing here?"

Elvis motioned toward Charley.

"What's going on? What's *he* doing here?"

"He wants to talk to you. He says it's important."

Jimmie's eyes shifted back to Charley. "You want to talk to *me*?"

"Yeah," Charley shouted through the loud disco music. "Can we get off this dance floor? I'd like to ask you a couple of questions without having to yell them at you."

Jimmie looked to Elvis for an explanation, but Elvis returned only a shrug of the shoulders. Turning back to Charley, Jimmie said, "Sure, follow me."

Jimmie led Charley and Elvis into the bathroom. "This is the quietest place in the bar." A loud groan coming from one of the stalls contradicted him.

Turning his attention back to Charley, Jimmie said, "I must say you're full of surprises. You're the last man on earth I'd ever expect to run into here."

As Jimmie's eyes moved down to Charley's chest, Charley began to understand why women were embarrassed when men ogled their breasts.

"You're Carmen Miranda," Charley said, effectively breaking the silence while diverting Jimmie's attention.

"Yeah. A cliché, I know, but I just love her. Did you ever see any of her films–*Weekend in Havana, That Night in Rio, The Gang's All Here*? Oh, I just love all of her films. But, then, I suppose you didn't come here to talk about Carmen Miranda, did you?"

Charley smiled and scratched his head. "No. Actually I came here to talk about Leah Gandalet."

"The Catwoman? What about her?"

"You said you just met her the night of the party. Were you being completely straight with me?"

Jimmie grinned. "Charley, now you should know I've never been straight." He chuckled.

"I'm serious, Jimmie. I need to know … were you telling me the truth?"

Jimmie shook off his laugh and studied Charley. "Yeah, why?"

"I just need to clear up a couple of things. Did she tell you anything that night?"

"I don't know … nothing unusual … just typical party talk. She came up to me, introduced herself, told me she'd come with this guy I'd met a few weeks ago."

Charley's eyes widened. "This guy she said she came with, who's he?"

"I met him at Baton a few weeks ago. He asked me to his table after my performance. He bought me a couple of drinks, complimented me on my performance and asked me out. We've gone out a couple of times since then. He's older, which I like, dark and rather distant. He's, how do I say this … *intriguing* I guess is the word I'm searching for." Jimmie lifted his brows for extra emphasis. "Anyway, you might have seen him. He was there at the party." Jimmie paused to think. "Oh, but you wouldn't have seen his face anyway. He was in costume and had a mask over his face. He was Batman."

"So, that explains Leah's Catwoman costume," Charley said. "I don't remember seeing anybody in a Batman costume, but that whole night is kind of a blur to me."

"Trust me. He was there."

Charley's eyes dropped to the floor as he contemplated his next question. After a couple of moments, he lifted his eyes and looked Jimmie square in the eyes. "Did he tell you *anything* about Leah?"

After thinking about it for a second, Jimmie shook his head. "No. I had invited him to the party, of course. He didn't tell me he'd be bringing anyone. In fact, I was surprised when he walked in with her. You know, I assumed he was interested in me."

"But he didn't say anything to you about her at the party?"

"No, in fact, we barely talked at all during the party. Of course, there were a lot of people there and I was the host. Come to think of it, I don't think I even saw him after Leah left with you. He sort of vanished into thin air. He didn't even say good-bye."

"And you haven't seen him since?"

"No." Jimmie stopped himself and looked curiously at Charley. "Why are you asking all these questions?"

"She's dead."

Jimmie's eyes widened. "Who's dead?"

"Leah. The Catwoman. Whoever she really is, or was ... she's dead."

Jimmie raised his brows. "You *know* this? Or you just *think* this?" Placing his hands on Charley's upper arms, he studied him.

"She's dead," Charley repeated. "They pulled her naked body out of a garbage bin in the alley just down from Bradley Place the other morning."

Jimmie's hands moved to his head with its hat full of fruit, slid down his face and stopped at his mouth. He'd seen the blurb in the paper about the body in the dumpster, but he'd never considered it would be anybody he knew.

"You're sure that was her?" He didn't wait for a response. "Of course, you are. You're a reporter. You'd never be in this place talking to me, of all people, if you weren't sure it was her." He pondered his next question. "So, then ... so then what? Do they know how she died?"

"Yeah. It'll be in tomorrow's papers. She died of a drug overdose. She took what she probably thought was ecstacy, but it was actually a much more dangerous kind of drug."

"There was a lot of ecstacy going around the party. Heck, I took some myself, and I'm still standing. You know, she could have gotten the drug from anybody that night–or anywhere else for that matter."

Charley nodded as his hands went to his temples and then drifted through his hair. "You must know Batman's name. What is it?"

"Yeah, of course. Harold Yarac."

"Do you know where Yarac lives?"

"No, like I said, we went out a couple times. But I never went to his place. We always met somewhere. We talked mostly. He seemed very interested in my profession. I could never really tell if he was really interested in *me* or my job."

Charley believed Jimmie. He thanked him and put out his hand to shake. Smiling, Jimmie shook the hand. "What ... no hug?"

Charley returned the smile. "Not for a man with a fruit basket on his head."

Charley turned toward Elvis, who was primping in the mirror. "Thanks for your help, too, Elvis."

Elvis caught Charley's eye in the reflection of the mirror. "Any time. And I mean *any* time."

Charley shook his head and chuckled. "I've got to go. People might start to talk."

"Charley, I hate to break this to you," Jimmie said in a rare display of seriousness, "but when it comes to people talking, we're the least of your worries. When that news story comes out tomorrow morning, there's going to be a whole lot of talk, and there's a good chance that talk might lead directly to you."

Charley nodded agreement. That same sinking feeling had been biting at him all day.

Chapter 7

How 'bout a cheese fry?

Charley came to a sudden stop outside the *Beat*'s office, gaping at the newspaper box. Pressed against the glass, in bold forty-two-point font, was the headline WOMAN'S DEATH LINKED TO COPYCAT DRUG. In smaller font was the sub-heading FOUL PLAY SUSPECTED IN CALL GIRL'S DEATH.

Although he knew that the story would be in the paper, seeing the headline somehow made it all the more real. This wasn't just another one of his bad dreams.

When he made his way inside, Lula Ann was positioned at the receptionist desk, face down in a crossword puzzle. Although she was old, she still had the ears of a watchdog. The creak of the door caused her eyes to roll up, and the sight of Charley's grim expression intrigued her enough to stir the pot a little. "Good morning, Charley," she said.

Since his first encounter with Lula Ann, Charley had steered clear of her. Truth be told, he thought she might be mentally unstable. There had not been even the usual office pleasantries exchanged between them, so her greeting that morning threw him off. "I'm sorry, Lula Ann, did you say something?"

Lula Ann cracked a wide, mischievous smirk. "I just said good morning."

"That's what I thought you said. Good morning to you, too." Charley started to glide by, but halted his movement and turned. "You know, I've been working here for a few weeks now, and this is the first time you've said good morning to me."

"Oh, really? I didn't realize that." Lula Ann didn't mind playing dumb. She knew that others thought her to be senile, and she used that to her advantage. "You looked … gee, I don't know … you looked worried, or something, when you walked in the door. Are you okay?"

Charley's eyes wandered. "Oh, yes, I'm fine. I've just had a bit of a bug lately."

"That's too bad. By the way, you should know, Buzz was looking for you earlier."

"For *me*?"

"Of course, don't ask me what for. Nobody ever tells me what's going on around here, but he was looking for you, and it sounded urgent."

A sense of doom overcame Charley. With a drop of his head, he slumped back to his desk while Lula Ann watched and giggled.

When he reached his desk, Charley grabbed a paper from the desk next to his, laid it out in front of him and started to scan Piper's story on the girl's murder. He was near the middle of the story when Buzz landed at his desk.

"Charley, what you got going today?" Buzz asked, hovering like a vulture.

"Not much. I was going to try to get caught up on a couple of things here and then head over to the courthouse."

Buzz had other ideas for Charley's day. The story of the call girl's death was gaining steam. Morning news radio and TV had picked up on it and the police chief had called a press conference for noon at City Hall. Piper was out checking into another angle on the story. That left Charley to cover the press conference.

This was when Charley should have asked Buzz if they could go to his office for a chat. He should have closed the door behind him and told him everything. Possibly it would have meant losing his job, but at least he'd have a clear mind. All he had to do was say, "I'm sorry. I can't take that assignment."

Although little was clear to him, he was certain that it would be wrong for him to take an assignment in which he had a personal stake–and it was becoming more and more evident that he did have a serious stake in what happened. His fingerprints were all over the place, and it was just a matter of time before detectives came knocking at his door.

If he just told Buzz the truth, he'd be throwing himself a lifeline. Instead, he dove straight into the ethically treacherous waters that were sure to lie ahead. There he was, once again, treading water, following that same ever-present path of self-destruction. In his wake, he'd put his career on the line. Piper had trusted him with information and Buzz had trusted him with a job. He'd repaid them with deception.

"I want to thank you for taking a chance on me," Charley said with a guilt-ridden conscience.

Buzz slapped him on the back. "Don't get all sentimental on me. Just keep those fingers dancing on the keyboards and you won't have to go back to dancing naked in front of those screaming women." He paused for a moment as a curious thought entered his mind. "Tell me, do they really scream?"

"Huh?"

"The women … do they really scream when you dance naked in front of them?"

Juggling lies was becoming a full-time profession for Charley. He'd almost forgotten about the lie that had gotten him the job in the first place. With a reluctant smile, Charley said, "Yeah, they do."

"So do you think they'd scream if they saw me naked?"

After completing an uncomfortable scan of Buzz and his hulking, hairy body, he said, "I'm pretty sure they would."

With five minutes to spare, Charley arrived at City Hall and raced to the elevator. He made his way to the sixteenth floor where a sign just outside the elevator doors pointed to the press briefing room.

Hurrying down the long hall, he made it to the press briefing room at 11:59 A.M. As he was about to walk in, a long, thick arm stopped him in his tracks.

"Got press credentials?"

Charley eyed the City of Chicago seal affixed to the breast pocket of the security guard. He looked up into a weary, weathered and dead serious face. Stepping back, Charley reached into his back pocket for his billfold and pulled out a temporary press ID.

Scrutinizing the ID, the security guard's facial lines tightened. "What's this?"

"That's my press ID," Charley explained, knowing now he shouldn't have put off getting his county-issued credentials.

When the guard asked if he had the county press ID, Charley bit his lip. "No, sorry I don't. Look, if you really don't believe me, you can call the *Beat* and they'll verify I'm supposed to be here as their press representative."

As the guard scrutinized the ID, his eyes repeatedly dashed back and forth between the picture on the ID and Charley's face. He turned to another guard and, after a brief discussion, took one last glance at the ID, and handed it back to Charley. "Go ahead. Go on in."

As he entered the press briefing room, Charley felt the anxious air of hungry reporters. Glancing around the crowded room, he spotted an empty seat at the end of the last row. He moved over there, sat down and pulled out his notebook. As he reached into his pocket for a pen, he felt a tap on his shoulder. Turning his head, he glimpsed beautifully manicured nails painted ruby red. His eyes turned up to see the angelic face of Grace Marks, reporter for Channel 2, who was more stunning in person than she appeared on TV.

"I'm sorry," she whispered, "but I thought I should warn you. You're sitting in Hundley Stockwell's seat." Channel 5's Hundley Stockwell was the dean of Chicago TV news and he had a robust appetite for both women and food, the latter of which showed in his corpulent three-hundred pound frame.

"His seat?"

"Yes. He always sits there. That's his news camera right behind you. He gets very irritated if anyone sits there. It's not like officially assigned to him or anything, but he treats it like it is."

Shaking his head in disbelief, Charley rose from the seat and walked around to where the beautiful Grace was standing. "Thanks for the warning."

"No problem. I just thought I'd save you some embarrassment."

As he breathed in her perfume, Charley introduced himself and admitted to feeling like he already knew her from watching her on TV. He hoped he didn't sound like a stalker.

"Glad to hear you're watching Channel 2. Who are you with?"

For a fleeting moment, Charley thought of lying, something that was becoming habitual. He could be a correspondent for the *New York Times,* which would certainly impress her, but if he were ever to be exposed as a fraud, he'd be subjected to endless ridicule in the newsroom, so, for a change of pace, he told the truth, explaining that he usually covered the courthouse and felt a little out of his element at City Hall.

Putting her right index finger to her luscious lips, Grace said, "Hubbs... I think I've seen your byline. You've done some good stuff for the *Beat*. I live up on the North Side, so I pick up the *Beat* pretty regularly."

With his ego positively stroked, Charley smiled and said thanks.

Grace smiled in return and then pointed at Hundley Stockwell as he entered the room. "Watch... he'll go straight for that seat you were just in."

Hundley's bountiful posterior spilled over on both sides of the chair, eliciting snickers from Charley and Grace. As they enjoyed the moment, Police Chief Gerald Matthews shuffled into the room, flanked by two other officers.

The fun was over. Duties called. As the chief made his way to the podium, Charley said a regretful good-bye to Grace and sought out an empty chair. Scurrying to the third row, Charley took a seat and opened his notebook just as Matthews tapped the microphone to quiet the din.

The tall, lean forty-two-year old had risen through the ranks to become the city's first black police chief. He was known as a no-nonsense, military-style leader. Although he had a resonant, powerful personality, he always looked uncomfortable in front of a microphone. As he prepared to speak, he cleared his throat. "Excuse me, I want to thank all of you for coming here today. I have a grief, er *brief* announcement to read regarding the Leah Gandalet homicide investigation. After reading it, I will take a few questions."

Charley's ears perked up when he heard the word *homicide*. As far as he knew, this was the first time the police had officially used that term in connection with Leah's death.

Matthews glanced uneasily at the crowd of reporters that had assembled before returning his eyes to the sanctuary of the prepared statement he'd drafted. "As you all know, Chicago police recovered the body of Miss Leah Gandalet from a trash receptacle in the vicinity of Halsted Street and Bradley Place on Sunday morning. As was reported in the newspapers this morning, an autopsy by the Cook County Medical Examiner's Office determined that the victim died officially of an overdose of paramethoxyamphetamine, also known as PMA. In addition, Chicago crime investigators have collected a semen sample from the body of the victim for analysis. Chicago crime investigators are also following up on a tip that was received through an anonymous telephone call. That's all that I have right now. Are there any questions?"

Hundley Stockwell skipped the customary raising of hands and shouted the first question. "Chief Matthews, you have labeled this a homicide. Does that mean you have reason to believe there is a perpetrator out there who provided the victim with PMA with the intention of killing her and then dumped the body after she overdosed?"

Charley wondered the same thing. Did the police know more than they were telling?

Matthews turned to confer with an officer behind him before he turned back to face the question. "We are proceeding with this case as a homicide investigation, at least until we have evidence that it is not. That is all I can tell you at this point. Are there any other questions?"

Hands flew up around the room. Matthews pointed to Douglas Gilmour, the *Herald* reporter who was seated in the first row.

"You said you're following up on an anonymous phone tip. Did this tip point to any specific suspect or suspects?"

Again, Matthews sought the aid of the officer behind him. Whispers were exchanged behind cupped hands until Matthews nodded and turned back to his audience. "No, the anonymous tip did not point to any specific suspect or suspects. The tip, however, did give us a possible lead as to the victim's whereabouts in the hours before she died. Investigators are just now starting to follow up on that lead, so I cannot say how good of a lead it is at this point. I'll take one more question."

Hands shot up around the room again. For the last two years, Matthews had been having a secret extramarital affair with Grace Marks, which explained how she seemed to scoop the competition with stories attributed to *an unnamed source in the top police brass*. This also explained why he picked her pretty hand out of the bunch.

"Chief Matthews, our sources are telling us the victim was seen at a party in an apartment building not far from where her body was found. Can you confirm or deny this?"

Matthews knew who her *sources* were, but there was nothing more he could tell her, at least not in public. "As I previously answered, we are following up on a lead as to where the victim was not long before her body was recovered. I cannot tell you anything more than that at this point in time. Thank you."

That was that. Charley had a haunting suspicion Matthews had just given Grace the old non-denial denial. If, as he feared, Grace was on target, detectives would soon be swarming his apartment building. The trail was getting closer to him–uncomfortably so.

From a pay phone in the lobby, Charley dialed Piper's pager number. Seconds after he hung up, Piper responded.

"Hey, Piper. It's Charley. I just got out of the press conference over at City Hall. Buzz wanted me to team up with you on the Leah Gandalet story."

"Hey, kid. Good. Buzz took my advice on this one."

"What's that?"

"Oh, I knew you were interested in this story and I didn't want to go out to City Hall, so I asked him to get you on board."

"Really? Buzz didn't mention that. Anyway, did you want to meet up somewhere and go over our notes?"

"Yeah, sure. I'm up in Wrigleyville, checking out some things. How 'bout if you meet me up here?"

"Sure, there's a diner called Salt & Pepper, at the corner of Addison and Clark. How 'bout I meet you there in, say, forty-five minutes?"

"That works for me, kid. I'll see you there."

Charley sat in a booth across from Piper, who was munching on a large plate of cheese fries while sipping a thick chocolate shake.

With his mouth full, Piper said, "Hey, kid, you want some of these cheese fries?"

"No thanks." Watching Piper gorge himself on grease had diminished Charley's appetite.

"Too bad, kid. This is good stuff." Another cheese-drenched French fry fell victim to Piper's insatiable hunger. "So tell me what you got."

Charley ran down the events of the press conference with special note of Grace Marks' question to the chief about the party and the apartment building.

"Damn," Piper said, "I was hoping I had the scoop on that one. Why am

I not surprised somebody in the department leaked that nugget to Grace Marks–probably a rookie cop who thought it might get him into her pants. All of the vets know better. They's all tried the same routine, and all without much success, mind you. Doesn't stop Gracey from finding a new sucker when she needs one." Piper was unaware of her liaison with the chief. "Oh, well, I'm pretty sure I'm at least a couple steps ahead of the beautiful Miss Marks."

Charley's ears perked up. "So you got something?"

Piper smiled crookedly. "Yeah, kid. I think so. Not sure what yet, but I think I got somethin'."

Charley's eyes grew wider. "Yesss…"

"The apartment Miss Marks was referring to is over on Bradley Place, just a few blocks from where we're sitting now, right next to where they fished the tramp's body out of a dumpster."

"I know where Bradley Place is. I live on that street."

"No kiddin'?" Piper lifted an inquisitive brow. "The apartment building where this party took place is named after the street."

"That's where I live."

A cheese fry stopped in mid-flight to Piper's mouth. "For real, kid?"

"For real."

"Huh." Piper dropped the fry back on his plate and eyeballed Charley. "Why do I get the funny feeling you know more about this than you've been telling me?"

Charley bit the inside of his mouth and with a circumspect eye confided that he'd attended the party in question.

"So you know the guy who threw the party–the fellow I spoke with earlier today?"

Piper was ahead of the game. That meant trouble.

"You mean Jimmie Dart?"

"Yeah, that's the guy."

"He lives across the hallway from me."

Piper tilted his head in puzzlement. "What's goin' on here, kid? You've been holdin' out on me."

"No," Charley retorted. "I haven't been holding out on you."

"But you knew more than what you were tellin' me, right? I mean you've suspected something all along, right? What is it, kid? Is it that goofy neighbor of yours? You think he had something to do with this?"

"No. I mean, I just don't know. There's something strange going on and I just don't know what to make of it. I'm caught up in the middle of something here and–" Realizing that he might have confessed too much, not only for his own good but for Piper's as well, Charley cut himself off.

"Look, Piper, you've got to trust me on this one. I really don't know any more than you do about all of this." This was only a half-lie. Although there were things he knew that he hadn't confided, there were many things he didn't know. Most notably, he didn't know how the girl he'd met ended up naked and dead in a trash bin. He only hoped that the answers were with someone else and not from within himself.

"I think there's something you're not tellin' me here, kid. But, and for what reason I do not know, I'm going to trust you, like you said. Just remember, we're partners on this one. We're sharin' the byline. If you come up with somethin' big, I had better hear from you before I read it in the paper."

"Deal." Charley breathed a sigh of relief. He'd bought a *little* time. Somehow he needed to clear himself, before all the walls he'd built came crashing down on him.

"I think you're a good kid, kid. That's the reason I asked Buzz to get you in on this story. If I'd known you were practically a witness to all this, I'd probably have thought better of it. But I got you aboard, so I'm gonna go on sailin' with you. Just don't fuck me. That's my number one rule of reporting. It doesn't matter if you're a source or another reporter. You fuck me and I'll make sure you fuckin' pay for it."

Charley nodded. Point understood.

"So, kid, it looks like we're in this together. How 'bout a cheese fry?" Piper moved his plate a bit toward Charley.

Charley glanced down at the plate and, with curled lips, gingerly scooped a fry. The warm, gooey cheese squished between his right thumb and index finger. For a moment, he gawked at it hanging there like a limp, lifeless body, and then with a tilt of his head, he closed his eyes, opened his mouth and let it fall in.

Chapter 8

Pissing it away

Leah returned to Charley in a dream. Perched on top of his body, she licked her chops. "We're not really complete strangers," she purred.

Her manicured nails turned into claws, which she used like knives on his chest, slowly carving tracks into his skin. Blood trickled out of the razor thin lines that trailed her claws, staining the sheets of the bed.

"Aaaahhhh!" The pain felt good to Charley–a relief after all he'd been through. Finally, he could feel pain.

Opening her mouth to display two long, sharp fangs, a wicked smile came to her face. After she bent her head, she pressed her soft, warm skin against his face. Her whole body rubbed up against him as her lips ran up and down his cheeks and down his neck. When she opened her mouth, her fangs sank into the side of his neck.

"Oooohhh!" Charley screamed in ecstasy.

Blood dripped from the side of her mouth as she gazed with devilish eyes. "This *is* what you want, isn't it, Charley?" she asked.

Charley awoke, shaking and in a cold sweat. So real, it all had seemed, as if she'd come back from the dead to haunt him.

Placing his right hand to his temple, he shook his head as his eyes searched in the darkness until they found the alarm clock. The dead of night had returned. Seven hours he'd been out.

For several minutes, he sat on the edge of the futon with his elbows resting on his upper legs and the palms of his hands covering his eyes. The tears wouldn't come.

The walk to the bathroom felt like a chore. Stopping at the head of the basin, he turned the faucet and stared into the mirror. Dark circles hung like nooses below his eyes. He bent down, cupped his hands and splashed cold water on his face. "You *really* gotta get your shit together, man," he said to the mirror image of himself.

As he studied his reflection, the events of the past two months played out before him like a horror film. He'd managed to make a mess of his life all over again. Somehow he'd have to fix it.

His thoughts turned to Lizzy. Why had he let her go? Why hadn't he called her? This answerless debate kept punishing him.

Charley vomited into the toilet. After he flushed, he removed his sweat-soaked clothes and sprayed deodorant over his body. From the closet, he pulled out a pair of jeans and a red Polo shirt and slipped them on. The time had come to confront Jimmie once again.

When he knocked on Jimmie's door, Charley knew what to expect. Elvis, wearing a black poodle bathrobe that wasn't tied in front so that it exposed his bikini briefs underneath, answered the door.

"Oh, it's you again. I suppose you're looking for Jimmie."

Charley nodded.

"He's out stalking at The Manhole again. Why do I get the feeling there's something going on between the two of you?" Elvis smirked at his tease.

"I can assure you there's nothing 'going on' between the two of us–and there never will be."

"Oh, please, Charley, lighten up. You're such a homophobe."

"I *am*?"

"*Yes*, you *are*."

Charley tried to be open-minded, but deep down he knew Elvis was right. Although he had no rational basis to be uncomfortable around gay men, he was.

Reading Charley's mind, Elvis tried to lighten the mood. "Just be careful out there," he said, shaking his index finger at Charley like a parent trying to make a point to a child. "There are a lot of naughty boys out there."

Charley smiled. "I'll be okay. Trust me."

Elvis examined Charley's attire. "You're right. No self-respecting homosexual male is going to approach you dressed like that."

"What?" Charley glanced down at his clothes. "What's wrong with this?"

Elvis returned a disapproving shake of his head. "You look like you never grew out of Garanimals."

"I suppose I should be shopping for clothes at Ann Taylor?"

Elvis threw up his hands in mock disgust. "Charley, Charley, Charley ... you can dress like a man and still have a sense of style."

"Well, I guess you'll have to take me shopping one day, but this outfit's going to have to do for tonight. It's not like I'm out to pick up any guys anyway."

"If only you could get so lucky," Elvis chirped.

Charley stood in front of the bouncer at the door to the back bar and, without prompting, started to remove his shirt. The shirt was halfway over his head when the bouncer interrupted him.

"Hey bud, what're you doin'?"

Through the cotton of the shirt, Charley uttered, "I'm taking my shirt off."

"I can see that, but why?"

"To get into the back bar."

"You don't have to take off your shirt to get into the back tonight."

"But last night..."

"That was last night. This is this night. The no-shirt policy doesn't apply tonight, but, hey, if you want to go shirtless tonight, too, I'm not going to stop you."

"*No,* I'll keep my shirt," Charley assured. A disquieting thought entered his mind. "There isn't something else I have to do to get back in there tonight, is there? I mean you're not going to tell me to take off my pants."

"No, you can go back there just as you are, but I'll tell you what, if you asked that question of anybody else in here, you'd be running around in your briefs. You're lucky you asked the one guy in here who's not gay."

Charley was surprised to hear that the bouncer was straight. "Thanks, for what I'm not sure. For not being gay, I guess."

"So you're not gay either, I take it?"

Charley shook his head. "No."

"So what are you doing hanging out at a gay bar?"

"Good question. I'm looking for somebody. I was told he'd be here."

"I see. You know, most straight guys won't come near this place. It's funny, just a couple blocks west of here is another world. It's all testosterone-fueled sports bars. The guys that hang out in those bars won't come near these places. If they happen to be walking by, they won't even look this way. They act like this doesn't even exist."

Charley returned a knowing nod. "You're absolutely right. I'm one of those guys, and a couple days ago, I wouldn't have been caught dead hanging out in a place like this. I'm curious how you ended up working here."

The bouncer smiled. "I'm an actor. In fact, you can catch me at The Annoyance Theatre, up on Clark. We've got a show playing titled *Coed Prison Sluts*."

Charley shot a dubious glance. "You're kidding, right?"

"No, I'm not. You should check it out. It's a pretty funny show. Believe it or not, it's the longest running musical in Chicago. Anyway, working in theatre, I've got a lot of gay friends, so I feel comfortable around gay guys. I needed a job and one of my gay friends told me that The Manhole was hiring, so here I am."

"You know I thought I'd seen everything after living in Berkeley for six years," Charley said, "but I've met some of the oddest people since I moved here."

"Welcome to *The Twilight Zone,* the dimension between Wrigleyville and Boys Town. So are you going in?"

"I guess so," Charley shrugged. "How much odder can it get?"

"Oh, it can always get odder."

Stepping into the darkness of the back bar, Charley scanned the room and gauged that finding Jimmie that night wasn't going to be an easy task. Deciding a drink might make the search a little easier, he worked his way to the bar and ordered a Tanqueray-and-tonic from a bare-chested bartender with a Fabio-style mane of soft curls falling to his shoulders.

When the bartender came back with the drink, Charley pulled out a twenty. As he handed the bill to the bartender, he leaned over the side of the bar. "Say, you wouldn't happen to know a Jimmie Dart, would you?"

The bartender raised an eyebrow. "Why do you ask?"

"I'm looking for him, that's all."

"You, too?"

"What's that supposed to mean?"

"Apparently Jimmie Dart is a pretty popular guy. You're the second guy to ask about him tonight, so I guess you've got some competition." The bartender smirked.

"You don't know him?"

"No. I'd never heard of him until tonight, but I'm kind of curious about him now."

Discouraged, Charley nodded and then gulped down the drink. The gin felt good going down his throat. When the glass was empty, he set it down on the bar. Emboldened, he took a deep breath and strolled into the crowd.

Preoccupied by his search for Jimmie, Charley didn't notice he was being stalked. Devon Trinidad's eyes lit up the moment they caught sight of Charley's clean-cut whiteness. Eyeing him standing at the bar, he licked his lips like a hungry tiger. When Charley moved on, he tailed him to the edge of the dance floor and sidled up next to him. Deciding it was time to make a move, Devon turned toward Charley. "Jawanna dahns, mahn?" he asked, in a buttery smooth Jamaican accent.

The pulsating beat of Donna Summer drowned out his words. Dejected, he frowned, his wide lips curling in the shape of a horseshoe. Hanging his head, he was about to walk away. Then a bolt of courage came to him.

Holding a vodka gimlet in his left hand, he reached with his right to tap Charley on the shoulder. With his hand inches from Charley, he was bumped from behind and his upper torso crashed into Charley's side, splashing his drink onto the back of his shirt.

"Oh, mah!" Devon was mortified by his own clumsiness. "Ahm so sorry, mahn. Here, let Devon clean this up." Devon brushed Charley's back in a panicked mode. "Oh, it's gonna be just like new, mahn."

Charley didn't see any end to the cleanup effort, which was beginning to rival that of the Exxon Valdez oil spill, so he intervened on his own behalf. "Hey, it's okay. I'm pretty sure it'll dry on its own."

"Yah, of course, you're right, mahn," Devon said, as he tepidly pulled his hands away, looking like a kid who'd broken a cherished vase. "Ahm, so sorry, mahn. Ah'll pay for de shirt."

"No, *really*, that's not necessary."

"Dry-clean?"

"What?"

"I'll have it dry-cleaned for you."

"No, that's okay," Charley said, returning his focus to the task at hand--finding Jimmie.

Standing with his arms crossed against his chest, staring at the back of a wet, red Polo shirt, Devon told himself that it was best to just walk away. At least then he'd have some semblance of dignity and self-respect. But he couldn't stop himself. Nudging next to Charley, Devon introduced himself and offered his hand and many apologies.

Charley offered a timid hand and told Devon his name, noticing that he was holding onto his hand for a longer time than customarily acceptable for a simple handshake. Add that to the wistful eye that Devon was giving him, and Charley was able to put two-and-two together. Still, Charley was caught by surprise when Devon asked him to dance. Although he'd heard the question, Charley's mind fumbled. "Huh?"

"Jawanna dahns?"

Charley decided it best to let him down gently. "I'm sorry, maybe some other time."

"Oh," Devon sulked. "I see."

This was all that Charley could take in one night. Jimmie was nowhere to be found, his shirt was soaked, and, to top it all off, he'd been propositioned by a man. As he made his way toward the exit, he felt a tap on his shoulder. *What now?*

"I can't believe you walked right by me without saying hello, Charley."

Charley analyzed the specimen. The makeup was impeccable and hid any evidence of the face behind it. After judging the height and frame, he asked, "Is that you, Jimmie?"

"What, you didn't recognize me?"

Charley shook his head. "Well, I guess the brunette wig, pillbox hat and pink dress threw me a bit. Are you supposed to be Jackie-O?"

"Yes, what do you think?" He twirled like a model on the catwalk.

"It's a little morbid for you."

"You don't like it? I chose it especially for you."

"For *me*?"

"Yes, I met you as Marilyn and now you get Jack's other love." He laughed wickedly. "Don't you think it has a certain kind of symmetry?"

"Are you okay, Jimmie?"

"Yeah, I'm fine. Can't I just have a little fun? You look at me as if you don't know me."

"You just don't seem yourself tonight."

"Oh, and you *know* the real me? You barely know me at all. How dare you judge me, you selfish little prick."

"*What?*"

His eyes turned wild, like a rabid dog. "You *heard* me."

"What's gotten into you?"

"What's gotten into *me*? Maybe it's what hasn't gotten into you. How would you like me to change that for you, Charley boy?" He placed his manicured hands on Charley's crotch and squeezed. "Oh, that's nice. You like that, Charley boy?"

Glaring, Charley shoved him away.

"Oh, Charley, you're nothing but a prick tease." He laughed like a mad hyena. "Waaah-haaa-haaa! Waaah-haaa-haaa!"

Holding his glare, Charley gnawed on the inside of his mouth. Rage grew inside of him–the kind of rage he'd felt only once before–until his temper boiled over and he unleashed a violent punch that landed square on the jaw.

As he fell back on the floor, a hush enveloped the bar, broken only by the sound of Donna Summer's moaning and groaning on the song, "Love to love you, baby."

Much of the crowd in the bar now had its collective eyes upon Charley. He felt like he was in a boxing ring, and everyone was waiting to see if his competition would get up from the floor. His victim, splayed out on the floor like a cartoon character, lifted his head and shot a curious smirk.

Charley stormed away in a huff. A kaleidoscope of feelings–anger, resentment, bitterness and embarrassment– ate away at him. As he tramped home in the cool night air, Jimmie's words played over and over again in his head, like a broken record. Odds were that he was intoxicated, be it from drugs or alcohol—but there was something disturbing about him, something Charley hadn't seen before. Maybe it was the look in his eyes. Or that wicked laughter. Whatever it was, he didn't know if he could face Jimmie ever again.

Charley made it back to his apartment at a little before midnight. At the door he paused for a moment, the thought of knocking on Jimmie's door having entered his mind. Electing to take the safe route, he pulled his keys out of his pants pocket and unlocked the door to his apartment. The apartment had become a metaphor for his life—small, dark and lonely. This was the first time he'd seen it in this way. The apartment seemed wrapped in nothing but misfortune and gloom.

What am I doing with my life?

After changing into his boxers and T-shirt, he went to the bathroom and pissed a long, heavy stream into the toilet. As he watched the urine hitting the water, the answer to his own question came to him: *Pissing it away.*

Chapter 9

What color bow would you like?

Charley awoke the next morning to loud banging on his door, something that was becoming an all-too-familiar and unwanted trend in his life. This was exactly how all of his trouble started in the first place. Turning his head on the pillow, he glanced at the alarm clock. It read 10:02 A.M.

As the knocking continued unabated, the events of the last evening all came back to him, like an unwanted guest.

Pulling the sheets away, he crawled out of the futon. As he stumbled to the door, sleep still in his eyes, he scratched his head and yawned.

The knocking persisted.

"Just a second," he called, as he scrambled for the door. When he made his way to the door and disengaged the bolt lock, he asked, "Jimmie, is that you?" Then, as the door inched open, he said, "I'm really sorry–"

The apology was not delivered to Jimmy but to two men he'd never seen before, or at least didn't recognize. Both appeared middle-aged and austere. One was tall and husky with shaved head while the other was short and stocky with hair combed-over to hide the baldness. Across the hallway, Charley eyed Elvis, peeping from the doorway.

"Can I help you, gentlemen?"

The tall one took the cue. "You are Mr. Charles Hubbs?"

"Charley. Yeah. Who are you?"

Now the short one jumped in. "Mr. Hubbs, we're detectives with the Chicago Police Department."

Charley gulped and his eyes widened.

The short one displayed a badge in his right palm for Charley to see. "I'm Detective O'Halloran," he said, and then motioned to his left. "This is my partner, Detective Bone."

Charley bit his upper lip. He knew the best way to get into trouble was to talk too much, so he tried to maintain an air of casualness. "So what may I do for you gentlemen?"

"Mr. Hubbs, do you know a Mr. James Dart?" O'Halloran asked.

The question caught Charley by surprise. "Sure, I know Jimmie. He's my neighbor. He lives right over there … right there, where you can see that sort of odd fellow poking his head out from behind the door."

In unison, the detectives turned their heads and caught Elvis poking his nose out from the doorway. The detectives had spent an hour with him before coming to visit Charley. Elvis blushed but didn't budge from his lookout post.

O'Halloran pressed on with Charley. "How well do you know Mr. Dart?"

"I don't know." Charley scratched his head. *Was Jimmie a suspect in Leah's murder?* "Not all that well, I suppose. I've known him now for a few weeks. What are you getting at here, detective?"

"Do you consider yourself a friend of Mr. Dart's?"

"Gee, I don't know. I suppose so. Or at least I thought we were friends … until last night."

Now Bone jumped in. "Last night? You *saw* Mr. Dart *last* night?"

"Sure, why?" Confusion bathed Charley's face.

O'Halloran took over again. "Where exactly did you see Mr. Dart last night?"

Perspiration began to collect on Charley's forehead. "I saw him at The Manhole, a gay bar just south of here."

"You said you thought you were friends *until last night*. What did you mean by that?"

Charley sought help from Elvis but none was forthcoming. Instead, Elvis shot back a scornful glare.

"I don't know exactly what I meant by that."

"But you said it. There must have been some reason for you making a statement like that. Something must have happened between the two of you."

Questions raced through Charley's mind. Why were they interested in his relationship with Jimmie? Why were they not asking about Leah? Where the hell *was* Jimmie?

"I guess I said that because we got into a fight."

The eyebrows on both detectives shot up at the same time, as if choreographed.

O'Halloran now took an accusatory tone. "You say you got into a fight?"

Charley nodded. "Yeah."

"What was the fight about?"

Laughing uneasily, Charley lifted his shoulders. "That's just it. I don't really know?"

"You don't know what?"

"What we were fighting about."

"But you *did* fight?"

"Yeah. He said some things that bothered me and he grabbed me by the crotch. I got angry and punched him."

"You *punched* him?"

"Yeah, he fell backwards on the floor. I walked away after that."

"And that was the last time you saw Mr. Dart?"

"Yeah. Why? What's going on? Is he in some kind of trouble?"

"Where did you go after you left the bar?"

"I went home and went to bed."

"What time was it that you saw Mr. Dart?"

"I don't know, about 11:15, I suppose."

"And what time did you get home?"

Charley scratched his head. "I'm not exactly sure. I walked around a bit. I think it was around midnight. What's this all about?"

Detective Bone dropped the big one. "Mr. Hubbs, Mr. Dart is dead."

"I ... I don't understand. That's just not possible. How–"

"We thought you might be able to elaborate for us on that one."

"What do you mean? What could I possibly know? I mean, how did he die? Was it a drug overdose?"

Exasperated, O'Halloran cut to the chase. "Mr. Hubbs, we think you know *exactly* how Mr. Dart died."

"No ... I don't. How could I possibly know? I mean yes, I did hit him, but he was very much alive when I left. If this was a drug overdose, I assure you, I had nothing to do with it."

"It was *not* a drug overdose, Mr. Hubbs." O'Halloran was growing impatient.

"I don't get it. How did he die then?"

"He was murdered, Mr. Hubbs," Bone said coldly. "His body was recovered from a bathroom stall at the bar where you admit to having engaged in a brawl with him."

The news rocked Charley like an electrical shock. All the questions now made sense. They thought he was a murderer–and not of Leah, but of Jimmie. The flesh of his face turned ghost white as his eyes darted back and forth until they landed across the hallway, on Elvis.

"Murderer!" Elvis yelped. "He's a murderer!"

Feeling numb, Charley could do nothing but shake his head.

O'Halloran shot an annoyed glance Elvis' way before returning his focus to Charley. "Mr. Hubbs, we have to ask you, did you kill Mr. Dart?"

Charley closed his eyes, breathed in deeply, and shook his head. "*No*. Like I said, when I last saw him, he was very much alive."

"But you admit to hitting him. How do you know that he was alive after you struck him?"

Charley gulped. "I saw him raise his head and, sort of, smirk. I have no doubt that he was alive. I walked away right after that, and haven't seen him since."

"Were there any witnesses to this fight?"

Charley lifted his hands to the temples of his forehead. "Yeah, there were tons of witnesses. The bar was packed and everything pretty much came to a stop when I hit him and he fell to the floor. I'm sure you could talk to anybody who was there last night and they would be able to verify all of this."

"Can you give us the name of anybody who was in the bar that night?"

Charley paused to think but then shook his hand helplessly. "No, I'm not a regular there. I was just there to see Jimmie."

"Did you talk to anybody other than Mr. Dart?"

Scratching his head, he remembered. "Yeah. Yeah. I talked to the bouncer ... and I talked to one of the bartenders. Oh, and there was some funny guy with a Jamaican accent who spilled a drink on me ... what was his name? I … I can't remember."

"I see. You said you walked around a bit after you left the bar. Did you stop anywhere on your way home?"

"No." Charley remained steadfast. "I just walked around. I was bothered by what had happened. I wanted to clear my head."

O'Halloran responded with a skeptical nod. "You're a reporter, right?"

"Yeah, why?"

"Nothing. I just don't like reporters. They're always stickin' their noses where they don't belong." He eyed Charley with cold determination. "You know what I think, Hubbs?"

Charley shook his head.

O'Halloran locked his eyes on Charley's and pointed his right index finger like a gun at his heart. "I think you killed him, and you can quote me on that."

The detectives had gone, but Elvis was still poking his nose out from the doorway.

Charley tried to persuade him to come out. "Come on, Elvis. We've got to talk about this. You've got to believe I had nothing to do with this."

"You murdered my best friend."

"No. I didn't. Why would I want to kill Jimmie? What motive would I have?"

"Jealousy. You wanted him all to yourself."

"That's crazy. I'm straight. You know that. What would I have to be jealous about?"

"I … I knew," Elvis stammered. "I shouldn't have let you go there alone. I just knew."

Elvis, having said all he could, slammed the door shut.

Charley was dumbfounded. For several moments, he stood there shaking his head and gawking at the door across the hallway. A phone call shook him out of the daze. Somehow he wasn't surprised to hear Piper on the other end. Somehow he also wasn't surprised that Piper had already heard the news about the murder. When Charley told him that the cops had just talked to him, he felt like he'd just put raw steak in front of a hungry hound.

"The cops were talkin' to you? What did they say? Did they tell ya anything?"

"Sorry to disappoint you, but the cops didn't tell me anything. They were here to question me, not to give me information."

"Question you? Why? Just because you lived next to the guy?"

"I suppose that's part of it. But there's a little more to it than that. I just can't tell you everything now. I wish I could, but I can't. Not right now anyway."

"Hey, you're not keeping something from ol' Piper, are you? Remember, kid, I'm the one who got you in on that last murder story."

"I'm not trying to steal a story from you. I know I owe you one. Hopefully, I'll be able to pay my debt to you soon. I just can't do it right now. I've got a few things to figure out."

"You're askin' for two things this old reporter doesn't have a lot of."

"What's that?"

"Patience and trust."

On his drive to work, Charley tuned his car radio to NewsRadio 1000 for its noon news. As he figured, the Boys Town murder was the top Top-of-the-Hour news. He thought the station could boost its listener base by advertising DEATH AND MAYHEM ON THE ZEROS, to go alongside its WEATHER AND TRAFFIC ON THE FIVES promo.

This was a disaster. Buzz would soon be leaning on him to assist Piper on the story. He had to dish up a plausible excuse for why he couldn't work on the story–other than the truth.

Just outside the office doors, he stopped cold in his tracks. The headline MURDER IN BOYS TOWN leaped out at him from the news rack. On closer inspection, he saw the story had been copyrighted and had Piper's byline. But how had Piper gotten the story in before the paper went to press?

Charley stormed through the doors and grabbed off the front desk the day's editions of the *Beat* and the two other Chicago dailies, the *Herald* and the *Sun*. Blowing by a wide-eyed Lula Ann, he tramped to his desk and, once there, tossed down each of the papers. Flipping through the pages of the *Herald* and the *Sun* with wild abandon, his search came up empty. The big dailies hadn't been able to get the story in before their deadlines. Piper had an exclusive. But *how* had he done it?

As described in Piper's story, Jimmie's naked body had been discovered in a bloodstained bathroom stall at The Manhole shortly after 11 P.M. He'd been pummeled and hanged by the skin on a coat hook. The story ended with the chronicling of a recent spate of physical assaults against gay men in Boys Town.

Charley leaned back away from the newspaper and put his hands to his face. His hands moved up his face and through his hair until they came to a stop at the back of his neck. The deadline was 11 p.m. The murder was at 11 p.m. The paper held its deadline for special stories, but that was reserved for stories that were known to be coming, like election night coverage. How could Piper have gotten the paper to hold its deadline for a murder–unless he knew it was coming?

Charley's thoughts were interrupted by Buzz bellowing, "Hubbs, get into my office! *Now!*"

The short trip to Buzz' office felt like a death march. When he reached the office, he found Buzz lounging back in his chair, wearing a mysterious, mischievous look on his face. On his lap, Buzz clutched in his large, hairy hands a single piece of paper.

"Close the door, Charley."

Following orders, Charley shut the door before timidly seating himself across from Buzz.

Now that he had his reporter's undivided attention, Buzz raised the piece of paper from his lap and held it in the air. "Charley, do you know what this sheet of paper is?"

"No, sir, I don't."

Buzz nodded. "No, I wouldn't expect you to know. This, Charley, is the entry application for nominations for the Pulitzer Prize."

Charley's eyebrows curled as he tilted his head a nudge to the right.

"Do you know why I'm holding this?"

"No, sir, I do not."

"Charley, please, stop calling me *Sir*. My name's Buzz. That's what everyone calls me."

"Yes, sir, I mean Buzz."

Buzz smiled. "Did you know, in my twenty-five years of journalism, I've never once filled out one of these?"

"No, I didn't know that."

"Of course you don't, but it's a fact–one I'd like to change."

"I don't know what you're getting at."

Buzz chuckled. "That's what I like about you, Charley. You get right to the point. Well, here's the point. Piper tells me you've got an inside angle on this Boys Town murder. He also tells me that there may be a link between it and that murder of the call girl. I want you and Piper to crack this open. I want to scoop the *Sun* and the *Herald* and everyone else on this one. This has all the makings of a big-time story and we're right smack dab in the middle of it--and Piper tells me you actually knew this fellow who was just killed over in Boys Town. This is too good to be true. Hubbs…"

Charley swallowed the saliva that had built up in his mouth. "Yes."

"I want this one. I want it wrapped up in a big bow with a page one exclusive--and you and Piper are going to bring it home for me."

Charley knew what he should tell him. "No. No way. Absolutely, no way." But he couldn't do it. He couldn't hurt Buzz, even though he knew, deep down, he might end up hurting him more by doing just this. So instead he answered with a question. "What color bow would you like?"

Chapter 10
Running On Empty

The puffy clouds of his breath floated out of his mouth as his legs churned on. Charley hadn't felt the Midwest cold in a long time, but now the crisp air felt good on his face. Lifting his T-shirt, he wiped away the sweat that, in spite of the thirty-five-degree temperature, still managed to bead up on his forehead.

He hadn't run in weeks, and it showed. After about four miles, his legs felt heavy and he was winded. He was, in both a literal and figurative sense, running on empty.

Yet he couldn't stop running. The reality was he hadn't stopped running since he left California. Yes, he was running away. Running from his past. And now what was he doing? Running from his present, too? They were two worlds that seemed headed on a collision course.

When he needed time to think, he ran. Now he thought of his past. Why couldn't he escape it? The more he tried to run from it, the faster it seemed to catch up with him. As he ran, the images of his past flowed back through his mind as if they were projected on a screen. There was the image of Dani, as she died in his arms, and then there was the image of him, cursing at God for taking her away from him.

Why couldn't he just let her go? Why couldn't the past just stay in the past? Why couldn't he start anew? Why? Why? Why?

So many questions haunted him. Too many of them unanswered. So he ran.

As he rounded a turn, he saw her first from a distance of about twenty feet, running toward him on the trail. He wasn't sure. Her hair looked longer, but it looked like her.

Ten feet–his heart raced even faster. Could it really be her?

Five feet–her eyes met his, or so it seemed. He was almost certain–it had to be her. He was about to call out her name–*Lizzy*–but then her eyes turned away, and her body brushed by his.

As he slowed to a stop and turned, he saw only an image of the back of her body. She didn't slow her pace.

He continued watching the image, as it faded into the distance, until he couldn't see it any longer.

Had it really been her? He thought he saw in her eyes a glimmer of recognition, but if so, why then did she just keep running? That was one he didn't want to think about. The pain was too much for him to bear.

Standing at the edge of the lake, he watched the waves pounding on the shoreline and thought about jumping in, ending it all. That would be one way to make it all go away. A splash of the cold lake water on his face triggered his memory of the promise that he'd made. Just moments before she died, Dani made him promise that he'd start his life over again without her.

"Promise me, Charley," she whispered in his ear, using her last breaths of life to salvage his. "It doesn't mean you have to forget me. It just means that you can be happy. That's all I want, for you to be happy."

She made him promise her, because she knew he wouldn't, or couldn't, do it on his own.

"I can't do that, Dani. I can't give up on you like that," he cried.

"Do it for *me* then," she pleaded, "if you can't do it for yourself."

Charley nodded his head, as tears flowed down his cheeks.

"Say it, Charley," she had urged. "Say, I promise."

At first, he shook his head, unable to make such a promise to her, but when he looked into those eyes and saw that look--the one that now haunted him–he broke down his defenses and said what she wanted to hear. "I promise."

With those two words, her eyes closed for the last time.

"Nooooooo!" His tears washed her luminous, silent face.

Then he turned on God, as he looked to the heavens above. "Damn you!

118

How can you call yourself a just and loving God? You take away a sweet, innocent, beautiful young woman, for absolutely no reason. What did she do to deserve this fate? Tell me that. Why her, Lord? Why not me? Tell me, damnit! Is this my punishment, to carry this burden for the rest of my life? Damn you! Damn you! Damn you!"

Winded and sweating from his run, Charley paced in the hallway outside the door to his apartment, debating whether to knock on the door across from his. He'd heard Elvis' words and seen the look on his face.

While he was running, he made up his mind. He needed to mend fences, to present his case. Yes, he was already thinking in terms of building his defense for trial.

Things looked bad for him. O'Halloran wouldn't stop his investigation until he had his man. As a reporter, Charley always tried to look at things objectively. He saw that the cards were stacked against him. The prosecution would be able to pull out any number of witnesses to the fight he'd had with Jimmie that night, and his dimwitted performance in front of the two detectives certainly wasn't going to help matters. Worst of all, he had no alibi. There was little doubt in his mind. The detectives were on a trail and it was leading to him.

Charley needed someone on his side. That's when he thought of Elvis, the one person left who might be able to help him. But there was something else pushing him toward Elvis as well. If he could somehow convince Elvis of his innocence, well, then, maybe things didn't look as bad as he imagined.

So he paced. What could he say? How could he convince him of his innocence? How should he present himself?

In his mind, he played out ways to begin his defense.

Okay, here's the deal Elvis ... I didn't do it.

Just let me explain. You know me. You know I couldn't do something like that.

He wasn't convincing—even to himself. But the time had come to face Elvis again, so he closed his eyes, took a deep breath, opened his eyes, made a fist with his right hand, and threw the fist twice on the door.

He gulped and waited—his eyes darting as he nervously tapped his feet. After waiting for a few seconds, he gave up and turned toward his door. As he fumbled for the keys in the pocket of his sweatpants, he heard the turning of a doorknob and the squeak of a door.

"Who's there?"

"Elvis?"

"Charley?"

"Yeah, it's me."

"I can't talk to you."

"Elvis, come on–open the door."

"Leave me alone."

"I just want to talk to you, to try to explain what happened."

"I can't talk to you. Leave me alone."

As Charley took a step toward the door, Elvis slammed it shut.

"Come on, Elvis. You're going to have to talk to me at some point. I promise you I didn't have anything to do with Jimmie's murder. I'm as sad and torn up about this as you are. If you'd just give me a chance to talk to you, I think you'd see that."

He waited. For fifteen minutes he stood in the hallway, but Elvis never reopened the door.

Many days later, Charley would learn that Elvis couldn't have come back to open that door. He was tied up–his neck wrapped around a noose that hung from the ceiling fan. A suicide note had fallen out of Elvis' hand and onto the floor. On it was written, *Jimmie, I'm coming to stay with you again.*

A heavy rain pounded on the windows while Charley tossed and turned on his futon, gazing at the ceiling fan hanging motionless above his head. He was thinking of how messed up his life had become when at ten minutes past midnight he was startled by a knock. Unaware that Elvis had gone to join Jimmie in the great apartment building in the sky, he had thought that maybe, just maybe, Elvis had reconsidered and had come to see him. This raised his hopes for a few brief seconds, until he opened the door and found Piper, clothes soaked and hair dripping, looking like a wet rat. Charley caught a whiff of beer and cigarette smoke, which the rain had been unable to wash away. "Piper? What are you doing here?"

"We've gotta talk, kid." Piper's body swerved as he spoke.

Charley turned his head away in an unsuccessful attempt to escape the foul smell of Piper's breath. "You're drunk."

"Damn right, I'm drunk."

"What are you doing here?"

"Like I said, we've gotta talk."

Charley nodded as he held onto the door gawking at Piper standing in a small puddle of rainwater.

"So are ya gonna let me in?" Piper didn't wait for an invitation as he pushed past Charley.

"Where's your furniture?"

"That's it," Charley said, pointing at the futon, which had been turned into his bed for the night.

Piper glanced Charley's way with a raised brow. "I'm beginning to wonder about you, kid." Charley nodded. "Do you have a closet?"

"Yeah, it's over there," Charley said, pointing to the opposite side of the room.

Piper sloshed over to the closet. "Well, at least you've got a closet. Hopefully there's nothing hidden in there I'm not supposed to find. You know, like dead bodies piled up in there or something." Piper guffawed.

Charley didn't see the humor. "No, there's nothing hidden in there, other than my meager wardrobe."

With the closet door obstructing Charley's view, Piper took a hand-size tape recorder out of his trench coat pocket before hanging the coat and closing the door. "Hey, kid, you wouldn't happen to have an extra towel around, would ya?"

"Yeah, sure." Charley strolled into the bathroom, where he pulled out a towel from the cabinet under the sink. As he did that, Piper turned the tape recorder on, placed it under the futon and positioned himself on the futon so that his feet would block Charley's view of the tape recorder. Moments later, Charley handed the towel to the still dripping Piper.

"Kinda wet out there," Piper said, drying with the towel. "Hey, I didn't wake you or anything, did I?"

"No, I couldn't sleep."

Piper nodded. "Huh. I bet ... the rain and all."

For a few moments, there was an uncomfortable silence, which Charley eventually broke. "So, you wanted to talk about something?"

"Yeah," Piper said, scratching his head. "Say, you wouldn't happen to have any beer, would ya?"

"Yeah, sure, Honker's okay?"

Piper nodded. "That would be great."

Charley walked into the kitchen. The refrigerator was bare except for two six-packs of Honker's in bottles and some catsup and mustard packets, leftovers from a late-night stop at Wrigleyville Dogs.

"Hey, you might want to get one for yourself, too," Piper barked from across the apartment. "I think you might need it, considerin' what I'm gonna be tellin' ya."

Charley gulped. What did Piper know? Taking Piper's advice, he grabbed a beer for himself. When he made it back to the living room, he handed one of the beers to Piper and took a seat next to him.

"You're not much into home decorating," Piper cracked.

"I don't need much."

Piper nodded and turned his beer-fogged eyes toward Charley. "We've got some issues to resolve, kid."

"Okay…"

"I really don't know what to make of you, kid. Either you're one dumb-ass, son-of-a-bitch, or you're playin' me for a sucker. I don't see any in between here, and either way you're fucked, in my book. I told you my number one rule. Don't fuck with me. Remember? I've gone along with your half-ass stories for a while now, but I'm not gonna go to bat for you much longer. You gotta come clean with me, kid."

"What do you mean?" Charley gnawed on the inside of his mouth, fighting to maintain a poker face.

"I think you know what I mean."

Charley rose from the futon and turned his back. "Tell me what you know," he challenged.

"No, kid," Piper fired back. "That's not the way it works. You're going to tell me the truth, and then if I'm satisfied, I'll tell you what I know."

"Okay," Charley sighed. The stalemate was broken. Charley cried uncle.

"Good." A sly smile crept on Piper's weathered face.

Charley told Piper everything, from the Halloween party to the knockout punch at The Manhole. "So that's the whole story," Charley said as he wrapped it up. He felt good to have released all that he'd been holding inside. "I'm sorry I didn't tell you all of this sooner."

"It's okay, kid." Piper smiled wryly. "I knew you'd tell me eventually. I'm just sorry I had to trick you into spillin' the beans."

Charley tilted his head a bit to the right. "Tricked?"

"Yeah, kid. I don't have anything. I made it all up. I've been puzzled by all of this for a while now. I was sittin' at the bar tonight, tryin' to piece it all together, but things weren't comin' together for me, so I came up with this plan to scare you into tellin' me whatever you knew. I'm not sure why, but I figured you knew more than you were tellin' me, so I turned you into the suspect. Now, mind you, I never really thought you were involved to the extent you're now tellin' me you actually are, but I thought, what the hell do I have to lose—you either tell me or you don't. I must say, kid, your story surprised even this old newshound."

Charley shook his head in disbelief. "So you really don't know anything?"

"Nada." A wide smile spread across Piper's face. "I feel kinda bad now—but not too bad."

"You shouldn't feel bad at all," Charley said. "I should have told you all this a long time ago. We're partners. I owed it to you to tell you the truth."

Piper took the last swig from his beer. "That's right … say, can you get me my coat out of the closet?"

Charley put his beer bottle down on the floor and stood. As he walked to the closet, Piper reached under the futon and grabbed the tape recorder. Lifting his eyebrows, he glanced Charley's way, pressed OFF and placed the recorder into his back pocket.

As Charley handed Piper his coat, Piper said, "I'm glad we're all out in the open now." Charley smiled.

"Me, too," Charley said. "Me, too."

Charley had an achy head and a rumbling stomach when he showed up for work the following morning. After Piper had left the previous night, he'd finished off the rest of the six-pack to help him sleep. Now he was paying the price. Glancing at the piles of phone messages, news releases and newspapers that had stacked up on his desk caused his head to spin, and when Buzz clamped a heavy hand on his shoulder, he came close to vomiting right there.

"Late today," Buzz kidded.

"I guess I overslept." Feelings of sickness and guiltiness now mixed together.

"Don't sweat it. You're usually here long before the rest of my reporters. Heck, you're usually here long before I'm even here. I only wish I had a few other reporters like you. How ya feeling today? You know, you didn't look so great the other day and, quite frankly, you still don't look so hot."

"Oh, I'm fine," Charley lied.

"So what you got goin' today?" The question dreaded by all reporters, especially one's that didn't have much of anything going.

"Well…" Charley's mind stuttered. He needed to come up with something to save him from being subjected to the *Buzz-saw*–the Russian roulette style Buzz used to dole out assignments. The general rule was *any* story was better than one dished out by Buzz.

"I've got a lot of stuff stacked up here. Oh, and I wanted to do some legwork on the Jimmie Dart murder investigation." Not bad. Not *good*, but not bad.

"That all sounds good…"

Oh, no. Charley knew what was coming–the dreaded Buzz-saw. "But I'm kind of short on copy today." That was journalistic mumbo-jumbo for a slow news day. Buzz needed filler for the next day's newspaper.

"We got a press release from the State's Attorney's Office," Buzz went on. "I'd like you to try to pull a story out of it. It doesn't have to be much, you know, just an eight- to ten-incher."

Charley nodded. "Sure, no problem, I'll get it to you by the end of the day."

"Thanks, Charley." Buzz slapped Charley on the back. "That'll be a big help."

Before even glancing at the press release, Charley created a new document on his computer and typed in his byline and the dateline for the story. This was old habit, dating back to his days as a cub reporter. It helped him get over the *hump*–the daunting task of starting to write a story. For Charley, the story couldn't start without the byline and dateline. So typing them onto the screen meant he'd already cleared the hump. No longer was he staring at a blank document on his computer screen. He had a starting point and that made the rest of the task of writing much easier.

After typing in the dateline, he scanned the press release, which the State's Attorney's public information officer had given the bland headline MAN GUILTY OF DRUG TRAFFICKING. Charley often wondered if the PIOs in the State's Attorney's Office held contests amongst themselves to see who could create the most lackluster headlines.

The release reported that a jury had deliberated just forty-five minutes before convicting a Lakeview man of leading a million dollar-a-year cocaine trafficking ring with ties to the Colombian cartel. Four paragraphs it had taken to *summarize* this information.

The rest of the release was a three-paragraph *quote* from the assistant state's attorney who prosecuted the case, James Monahan. Charley knew that the words attributed to Monahan never came out of his mouth but were the fictional creation of a PIO.

Charley enjoyed the game of *Guess the Author*. Each PIO followed a basic template. They always made sure to give appreciation to the jury for its "hard work and careful weighing of the facts," and there was the requisite salute to State's Attorney Richard Bullock and his "continuing fight to rid the city of crime and drugs." Each PIO also had his own trademark and Charley had developed a keen eye for spotting the clues as to the identity of the anonymous PIOs. For instance, he could discern that Tim Pappadopolous had authored the release about the cocaine trafficker by his mention of the gender makeup of the jury—seven men and five women. Charley didn't understand how this was relevant to the story, any more than say a breakdown of the jury by racial or age categories, but apparently Tim Pappadopolous did, because he included the gender breakdown in *every* release he wrote in which there was a jury verdict.

After reading the release, Charley picked up the phone and dialed the direct line for James Monahan. As he figured, Monahan didn't answer. Most likely, he was in court. The call jumped to a secretary with whom he left a message to have Monahan call him.

After hanging up, he took a deep breath. A potent mixture of anxiety and a nasty beer hangover had him feeling sick all over again. Trying to put his sick feeling out of his mind, he placed a call to the press officer for the Chicago Police and ended up speaking with Jill Ryan, one of the friendlier press officers in the department. She informed him that there was no new information to give out in regard to the death of Jimmie Dart, only that the investigation was continuing. This didn't surprise him, but he continued to hold out hope that a killer would be found so that his life could return to some sense of normalcy. Fear that he could be blamed was starting to take a toll on his ability to function.

After hanging up the phone, he sorted through the piles that had stacked up on his desk. He skimmed through the newspapers and his mail and phone messages, but found it difficult to concentrate.

At a quarter to one, he put his fingers to the keyboard and started writing a skeleton version of the PIO release. Later, he'd fill in any quotes or additional information received from Monahan.

Usually writing a skeleton story—especially one derived from a press release—took him no time. Mostly it was just re-writing the release to make it something people would actually want to read. Today was a different story, however. He couldn't get his fingers moving. They sat frozen on the keyboard, as his eyes fixed on a computer screen with only a byline and dateline for a story that was supposed to follow the dash.

Occasionally he tapped his fingers on the keyboard, thinking that if he at least moved his fingers words would eventually appear. They didn't.

He looked at his watch. The time was now a quarter past one. Although he'd skipped breakfast, he wasn't hungry. The way he was feeling, he didn't know if he could stomach food anyway.

Some time away from his desk might do him some good. He certainly wasn't getting anything accomplished *at* his desk, so he stepped out of the office and started walking, not even thinking about where he was going. At some point, he blacked out.

When he regained consciousness, he found himself standing back outside the doors to the *Beat*. How he'd gotten there he didn't know. Had he even left? For all he knew, he could have been standing in the same spot for the last hour.

Back at his desk, he tried to shake off his latest blackout spell. As he stared at his byline, he realized that writing had become a chore for him—

something Dani had told him it wasn't supposed to be. He managed to fight his way through the rest of the skeleton story when the phone rang. On the other end was Monahan, the state's attorney who'd handled the drug case.

With his ear to the receiver and his fingers typing Monahan's words onto his computer screen, Charley didn't notice the two plain-clothes detectives who'd walked through the front door and talked to Lula Ann, who pointed them towards his desk.

The detectives strode through the newsroom like they owned it, until they came to a stop beside Charley's desk.

The shadow of the detectives hovering over him caused Charley to raise his head. He recognized them as the same ones who'd interrogated him at his apartment. As he eyed them, Monahan was going on and on about the prosecution of the drug case.

"Hey, Jim," Charley interrupted, "would it be all right if I called you back in a little bit?" Before Monahan had a chance to respond, Charley set down the phone and peered up at the detectives. "Can I help you, gentlemen?"

Detective Bone brought the news he'd feared was coming. "Mr. Hubbs, you are under arrest for the murder of James Dart." The detective showed Charley the cuffs.

"Do you really have to?" The eyes of the newsroom were all on Charley.

"It's procedure," Bone said. "Nothing personal." Charley knew otherwise but obeyed. The detectives had made it clear to him before that they didn't like reporters. Taking one out of a newsroom in cuffs was probably a pants-buster for them.

Viewing the scene played out in his newsroom through the glass of his office, Buzz slammed the phone down and hustled to Charley's rescue. "What in the livin' hell's goin' on here?" Buzz glared like a cat whose tail had just been stepped on.

"It's okay," Charley said, knowing that it wasn't.

"Talk to Piper. He'll know what this is all about."

Embarrassed and ashamed, Charley hung his head as the detectives escorted him out of the newsroom. The nightmare was now all too real.

Chapter 11

A wild ride

After just two hours in the police station lockup, Charley was feeling stir-crazy. How could people spend months, years, or a lifetime behind bars? They deal with it. They adapt.

Or they escape.

Escape. Charley chuckled at the thought. The idea was ludicrous, but for some reason, he couldn't kick the thought, and the more it stuck, the more he began to think … maybe.

He'd never thought of himself as bold, brave or daring, and maybe he wasn't. Maybe he was just being foolish, but he kept coming back to the same question. What did he have to lose? The answer was always the same. Nothing.

He'd been around the courts long enough to know the odds were stacked against him if his case went to trial. Cook County prosecutors boasted of a ninety percent conviction rate. That left him with a ten percent chance of acquittal. The odds in his case might be a tad better than that. The case against him would be circumstantial–unless the police had evidence that he wasn't aware of, a possibility he didn't want to consider. A jury only had to find him guilty "beyond a reasonable doubt." The evidence that would be put forth would show he'd publicly fought with Jimmie shortly before he was found dead, which would raise a lot of eyebrows in the jury. As he weighed it in his head, Charley put the odds of acquittal at no better than fifty-fifty.

129

Could he risk his life on what were, in a best-case scenario, fifty-fifty odds? No, for once in his life, he needed to be proactive. He was tired of letting fate–or pure bad luck–control his life. The path his life had taken needed to be reversed.

How could he pull it off? His only knowledge of jail escapes came from movies like *Escape from Alcatraz*, and he was no Clint Eastwood. Courtroom escapes, however, were a different matter. He'd hung around courtrooms long enough to have witnessed a few defendants make the break. Of course, he also knew the success rate was next to zero. Most didn't even make it out of the courthouse, and those that did manage to bust out the courtroom doors were usually rounded up not long after they had gotten their brief taste of freedom. One time a courtroom escapee ran out of the courthouse and right into a police station.

Knowing all of this, he could easily, and maybe should have, cut off any thought of escape right there, but he couldn't help but think that maybe, just maybe, there was something to be learned from these failed attempts. After all, he already knew what *not* to do from witnessing and reporting on others who'd tried to bust out of the courthouse. He also figured that most defendants who bolted from a courtroom had done so without a plan or scheme, acting on impulse, pure adrenaline, fear, or all of the above. The results were thoughtless, reckless escape attempts, doomed to failure. Finally, and this was a big one in his mind, he knew all the ins and outs of the courthouse like the back of his hand. After all, he spent most of his workdays there, so he knew the fastest route from Point A to Point B, and he knew all of the secret passageways, or at least he thought he did.

As he added it all up in his mind, he had three distinct advantages over others who'd attempted courtroom escapes. That was enough to make him think he had a chance, and given his precarious state, a chance was all he needed to believe it was worth the gamble.

Having decided that there was at least a chance he could do it, and that he didn't really have anything to lose, he set out to figure out how to do it. This, for Charley, did not come easily. Risk-taking and lawbreaking went against his nature. While some people liked life on the edge, he preferred life a county away from the edge. His job reflected his nature. As a courts reporter, he often felt like a peeping Tom, with the courtrooms providing the window through which he could peer into the lives of people who had crossed over to a side he'd never been on.

Thinking of his job made him for the first time consider what it would be like when he was brought into a courtroom to face the charges that had been brought against him. He anticipated a full-blown media circus, knowing that Jimmie Dart's murder was already big news and that the arrest of a reporter, one who had been covering that murder for a local newspaper, would fuel all kinds of gossip and innuendo. Many of his peers would be licking their chops, hungry to get in on the story. Of course, if the roles were reversed with any of them, he'd be salivating for the story just like they were–a thought he found difficult to digest.

As he thought about all of this, he came to the realization that his best chance for escape would be during his first court appearance for a bond hearing. The anticipation at that point would be the greatest, as he'd be ceremoniously brought out for the first time and announced as the killer–*alleged* killer, he corrected himself–of Jimmie Dart. The courtroom would be abuzz, packed with reporters, lawyers, friends of Jimmie Dart, gay activists, and curiosity seekers.

What would be the last thing all of them would expect? An escape. A wicked smile arose across his face as he pondered the idea. The bond hearing would allow him to play his greatest card–the element of surprise.

Always the reporter, he thought of the headlines his escape would make. His smile widened further. Truth be told, he'd kill for a story like the one he was plotting in his head. Of course, that's what many in the courtroom would be thinking he did, indeed, do.

He mapped out in his mind the path from bond court to the doors leading out of the courthouse. This was another factor in his favor. Bond court was held in the courtroom closest to the courthouse exit. A hundred-yard dash and he'd be out the doors, assuming the deputies from the Cook County Sheriff's Department were caught off guard and didn't catch him first–and that, he knew, was a rather big assumption.

Even if he did manage to make it out the door, where would he go? The area around the courthouse would be swarming with cops as soon as the escape alarm sounded. On his feet, he'd be a sitting duck. They'd round him up in no time and toss him back in jail, and his fate would be sealed for good.

That's when he concluded that he couldn't carry out his plan alone. He needed an accomplice–one with a car.

Who would help him? He sulked at the thought. The answer, to him, was clear. Nobody. He couldn't ask Buzz or Piper to get involved. They were more involved than they ever should have been, especially Piper. Not to mention that they had a job to do, a job that included reporting on his trial. The only other person that came to mind was Lizzy, but he'd shut her out of his life. There was no way he could open that door again.

Or could he? The more he thought, the more he realized that Lizzy was the perfect accomplice. Nobody would tie them together because nobody knew there was a connection between them.

There was one major glitch in his scheme. How could he ask her to put her neck on the line for him after he'd walked out of her life? She'd be risking jail time for him. No, he didn't think she'd do that for him, and he didn't think he could ask her to do it.

There. Case closed. The whole idea was ludicrous anyways.

He lie on the jail-issue cot, staring into the darkness. Hours passed, and with each passing hour, he felt more alone, more scared–and more desperate.

At 11:35 P.M., he sat up, realizing what he needed to do.

Dickie Boyle, the desk sergeant, and Tommy Crawford, a veteran beat cop, were laughing at a dirty joke Crawford had just told when they heard a mysterious clanging sound. Their laughter came to an abrupt halt as they both looked at each other with puzzled eyes and tried to make out the sound. "What the hell's that?" Crawford asked.

Boyle raised his shoulders. "Sounds almost like it's comin' from the lockup."

"You know, I think you're right. That guy they charged with knockin' off that drag queen's back there, ain't he?"

"Yeah, the reporter. What's his name? Umm ... oh, Hubbs, I think the name is. I checked on him about an hour ago and he was in the cot. I thought he was down for the night."

The clanging continued unabated.

Boyle and Crawford listened in for a couple of minutes until Boyle looked at Crawford. "So, you think we oughtta check it out?"

Crawford was off duty in thirty minutes and gave Boyle a look that clearly said he wasn't about to budge. Boyle, irritated at Crawford's indolence, decided he'd better check it out himself. "So, can you *at least* keep watch here at the desk while I go check it out?"

Crawford looked down at his watch. "I suppose. But don't dilly-dally. I'm outta here in thirty."

Boyle felt like he'd just asked Crawford to help him move cross-country. "Just stand there and answer the phone if it rings. I'll be right back."

His white hair and protruding belly reflected how long Boyle had been a Chicago cop. Next year would be his thirtieth–and final–year on the force, and he was looking forward to retirement in the Florida Keys. In thirty years, he'd seen just about everything in his career–and he didn't need any surprises now.

When he got to the lockup, he saw Hubbs standing at the cell door, holding a tin cup.

"What the hell do you think you're doin'? This isn't Mayberry, you know."

"I didn't know how else to get your attention."

"There's a buzzer right over there," Boyle said, pointing to a black button on the wall, next to the cot. "That's for emergencies. I hope this is an emergency."

"Oh, I don't know if it's an emergency or not. I just need to make a phone call."

"Didn't you get to make a call when they booked you?"

"Yeah. No. I mean, not exactly."

"What exactly is *not exactly* supposed to mean?"

"I mean they offered to *let* me make a call. I just didn't have anyone to call at the time."

"And now you do?"

Charley nodded. "Yeah."

"And this is important?"

"Yeah."

Boyle knew he didn't have to let Charley make the call, and that, technically speaking, he'd be breaking procedures by allowing him to do so, but for some reason, which he couldn't quite figure out, he felt obliged to allow this request.

"All right," he relented, "but you'll have to keep it short. Five minutes. That's all I can give you, and *don't* make me regret this."

"Yes, of course. Thank you."

Boyle eyed the inmate cautiously as he put the key in the cell lock. "Follow me."

The sergeant led Charley to a closet-sized room, which was empty except for a chair, small table and telephone. He opened the door and motioned the inmate in. "Remember ... five minutes."

Charley nodded, walked in and sat down at the table. Hearing the door close behind him, he turned and noticed Boyle watching through the glass window of the door. Boyle raised his right hand and displayed his four fingers and thumb.

Charley nodded again and turned back to face the phone. His heartbeat raced. Would she be home, and if she were, what would he say to her and how would he say it all within five minutes?

He turned back and glanced at the sergeant, whose impatience was showing in his weary eyes.

The time had come–now or never.

In his mind, he'd done this numerous times over the past two months. The number he knew by heart. The first six digits he dialed at a rapid pace, but on the final number he stalled.

One more time he reminded himself he had to do this and his index finger hit the final number. Holding his breath, he listened as the phone rang. Once. Twice. Three times. *She's not home.*

On the fourth ring, however, there was a click on the other end followed by a tired "Hello."

Her voice melted his heart. "Lizzy?"

A slight pause followed before she realized. "Charley?"

"Yes, Lizzy. Are you awake?"

"Yes. Well, I am now."

"I'm sorry for waking you." There were so many things he wanted to apologize for, but time didn't allow for that. "Look, Lizzy, I'm in trouble and I need your help."

"Trouble?"

"Yes, a *lot* of trouble. I'm in jail right now."

"*Jail?*"

"Yes, I've been charged with murder."

"*Murder?*"

"I'm completely innocent. I can't go into it all right now, but I really need your help."

"Of course, but what can *I* do?"

As he laid out his plan, he barely had time to catch a breath let alone think of what might be running through her mind. "Did you get all that?"

"Yes. Well, I think so."

"I know I've gone over all of this kind of fast for you, and I owe you a lot of explanations, but, like I said, I just don't have enough time for all of that right now. What I need from you is to tell me right now whether you'll do it or not. Please know, if you say no, I'll completely understand. I'm asking you to do something that's very illegal. I realize that. I just don't think I'm going to be able to prove my innocence unless I'm out of jail, and I don't think I can get out of jail without your help."

"Charley, I ... I ... I just don't know."

The pain echoed in her voice and shot straight to his heart. There was a knock on the door, and Charley turned to see the sergeant holding up his index finger, signaling that he was down to his last minute. Time was of the essence.

"Lizzy, I'm *really* sorry ... for everything. I just really need for you to tell me one thing right now, and that is, will you help me?"

The question was met by silence. A knock on the door served notice that time was up.

Charley's hands trembled as he eyed the sergeant through the window of the door. Hope was fading fast.

"Okay."

Her reply was subdued, lacking in conviction, but still music to Charley's ears. She'd said the word he wanted to hear and he breathed a sigh of relief. "Thank you, Lizzy. Thank you. I promise I–" The sergeant pressed his finger on the phone line, disconnecting them.

As he was being escorted back to his cell, Charley thought about the promise that was left hanging in the air. What he was going to promise her was that she wouldn't regret it. As he thought about it, he decided it best he hadn't been given the chance to complete his promise, because he knew it was a promise he couldn't guarantee he'd be able to keep, and he'd already let too many promises in his life go unfulfilled.

The sun was just starting to rise across a cloudless sky above the chilly, late-November waters of Lake Michigan when Sergeant Boyle pulled out his pocket watch and saw that it was time.

As he strolled to the lockup, he twirled the key to the cell and whistled the tune, "My Irish eyes are smiling."

When he reached the cell door, he peered in on his inmate. There was no sign of movement. In a thick Chicago Irish brogue, he barked, "A'riiiise and shiiiine."

Charley stretched his arms as his eyes struggled to open. Morning had come much too early. After he mustered up all of his strength just to lift his head out of a nearly decomposed pillow, he coughed, "All right. I'm up already."

"Five minutes," Boyle boomed back. "Your limo's outside waitin' for ya." He snickered at his own words.

Charley dragged himself out of bed, stumbled to the sink and splashed cold water on his face. The day of reckoning had come.

He grimaced in pain as he bent his neck down to look in the mirror. When he caught sight of his face, he cringed. The dark circles under the eyes, the mussed hair and the six o'clock-in-the-morning shadow across the lower part of his face reminded him of Otis Campbell, the drunk who always slept it off at the Mayberry police lockup.

In a few hours, he'd be in a courtroom. If all worked as planned, he'd be seeing Lizzy for the first time in two months. How to make himself presentable? He combed his thick, grainy hair with his fingers and tucked in his button-down denim shirt into his charcoal-brown slacks. The wrinkles in his shirt he tried to iron with his hands, but he soon surrendered and deemed the shirt a lost cause. As he washed his face, he heard a key inserted into the lock of the cell and turned to see the cotton ball white hair that floated atop Boyle's head like a lonely cloud.

"Time to go," Boyle said, as he pulled open the cell door.

Charley nodded and walked to the door. As the sergeant cuffed him, he said, "You could have fluffed the pillow a little for me."

"Whatchya think this is, the Palmer House?" Boyle sneered.

Charley smiled. "By the way, thanks for letting me make that phone call last night."

Boyle now turned cautious and puffed out his rosy, round cheeks. "What phone call?"

Charley was caught a bit off guard by Boyle's response, but it didn't take him long to read Boyle's icy veteran-cop eyes. The phone call was off the books, not to be talked about.

Once they had a silent understanding established, the sergeant escorted Charley outside the doors of the police station to a paddy wagon parked on Addison. "This is your limo, Mr. Hubbs. I suspect you're in for one heckuva wild ride."

Charley stepped clumsily up into the wagon, nearly slipping on the shoelaces of his sneakers. Once safely in, he turned to Boyle. "I suspect you're right, sergeant," he said, a hint of doom in his voice. "I suspect I am in for one helluva wild ride."

PART II
Season of Hope

"What a great day for baseball. Let's play two!"

                                                   - Ernie Banks

Chapter 12

I Always Get My Man

Curled in the back seat of his car, Charley slept restlessly, his fingers twitching like those of a Texas gunslinger at sundown.

At 4:15 A.M., he was awakened, shivering and disoriented. A couple moments passed before he regained his bearings. For over sixteen hours, he'd been cooped up in the cramped quarters of his Hyundai.

His ears zoned in on the tapping that had wakened him. Somebody was knocking on the garage door. *She'd come for him.* The thought went through him like an injection of adrenaline.

Springing from the car, he raced to the door. As he was about to lift the door, a dreadful thought occurred to him. *What if it was the cops?* If it were, he was trapped.

His fears—at least those that concerned the cops—were washed away when he saw her. His instinct was to rush toward her and wrap his arms around her, but he restrained his impulse and offered nothing more than a vague smile. She wore a blue Cubs cap and a matching nylon jacket—and the same sad eyes he'd seen in the courtroom the day before.

"Come on," she said, benignly. "We'd better go."

He followed her, leaving his car behind, afraid to ask where she was leading him.

They walked in silence for a block, until they came to a white Volkswagen Beetle. Lizzy glanced Charley's way, careful not to reveal her feelings. Out of her jacket, she removed the car keys and unlocked the passenger door. She left the door closed and walked in silence to the other side of the car.

Driving in the darkness of morning, she kept her eyes glued to the road. Truth be told, she wanted to hurt him. She wanted him to know what it felt like. She wanted…

"I had a dream," Charley said, breaking the painful silence.

Lizzy turned her head and glanced at Charley, then returned her gaze to the road.

"When I was wakened, by your knocking … I had been dreaming. I remember being at a computer terminal. I couldn't see my face. In fact, all I saw were my hands, on the keyboard, and my fingers pecking away at the keys, and then I looked up at the monitor and saw what I'd typed."

Lizzy shot another glance Charley's way.

"Grandstroke. The same name … it was all across the screen. Nothing else. Just that."

Lizzy swerved the car to the side of the road and slammed on the brakes. The upper torsos of both jolted forward before the seat belt restraints caught and threw them back.

All of her feelings, simmering for so long, boiled over. "Charley, what the hell does this … this … this crazy dream have to do with anything? Why do you tell me this? I mean, really, it would seem that you should have a lot of things to explain to me … and all you do is talk about this crazy dream. What the –" Exasperated, she threw her hands up.

There were so many things to apologize for. He'd caused so much hurt and now had gotten her involved in his troubles. Charley didn't say he was sorry, though. Instead, he told her she was right.

There was so much for him to explain, and he'd started to do just that. She just didn't know it yet–and maybe he didn't, either.

After parking the car about two blocks from her apartment, Lizzy removed her cap and turned to Charley.

"You'd better wear this, and pull it down so that it covers part of your face."

Charley did as she said, then followed her in silence to her apartment. He'd told her in the car he would try to explain it all to her, but he knew that would not be possible, if only because he couldn't explain it all himself. There were things she needed to know, things he could tell her, things he'd been too afraid to tell her before. Discussing these things wouldn't be any easier for him now than they were before, and, more than anything, he knew that there was a real possibility after he told them to her, she'd leave him forever.

"Would you like coffee?" Lizzy didn't know how to act in front of him. The comfort level they'd shared before had vanished. Now she saw him in a different light. She felt awkward and shy–feelings that went against her nature. There were so many questions she had that she didn't know where to begin.

"Thanks, but no. I … I don't drink coffee."

"Oh. I didn't–" She turned away, hiding the tears that had welled in her eyes.

"Liz…"

With her back to Charley and arms crossed against her chest, Lizzy took a deep breath, curled her lips, and turned to face him again. "What?" Her eyes felt like burning embers.

"The dream I told you about…"

"Yes."

"Grandstroke, I know that name. But I don't know how."

"I don't understand."

"I don't, either. Not completely, anyway. But I think I have to find out who Grandstroke is if…" Charley lowered his head as he paused for a moment to collect his thoughts, then he looked Lizzy in the eyes. "If I'm going to find who I am."

"What? You're Charley Hubbs." Lizzy looked curiously at him. "*Aren't* you?"

"Yes. But, Lizzy, something happened to me. Something I haven't told you about. Something I don't really know if I can adequately explain to you, and it's not that I don't *want* to explain it all to you, it's just that I can't, because I can't explain it all myself."

"Go on…"

"I have these spells."

Lizzy's eyes widened. "Okay, now you're scaring me, Charley. What kind of *spells* are we talking about?"

"I black out. It's happened a couple times since I came to Chicago. I think it might have happened to me before I came here. Sometimes it's just for a minute or two. Other times, it's longer."

"So, what, exactly, are you trying to tell me, Charley?"

Charley gulped. "I can't tell you for certain that I didn't kill him."

"The man you're charged with murdering?"

"Jimmie Dart. Yes. And there's another murder, which is unsolved, which I may be responsible for as well."

Charley covered his mouth with his hand, as if trying to conceal his own admissions. Seeing the fear in Lizzy's eyes pained him, but he knew he had to tell her everything, no matter how much it hurt or scared her. If he didn't tell her, he couldn't ask her to help him.

"Listen, Lizzy…" He reached for her and she backed away. She wouldn't take his hand, either. "I'm telling you all of this because, because … because I want you to know everything. I *need* you to know everything. I don't *think* I killed these people. I just can't say for *sure* that I didn't, and I knew that none of this would hold up in court. Don't you see, I had to escape in order to find out for myself. I needed to prove to myself that I didn't–*couldn't*– have done these things."

Lizzy turned away, shaking her head.

"Look, I know this must all sound crazy to you."

Lifting her eyebrows, Lizzy tilted her head back, a sign that she'd heard about all she could take. She *did* think he was crazy, and she was beginning to think she must be crazy, too. Not only had she allowed herself to be convinced by him that she should help him escape from court, now she was allowing him to spout his crazy bullshit. How long would it be before the cops would be digging up her precious body parts from some forest preserve? Just one of these *spells,* and she'd be nothing but rotting, decaying bones.

As those thoughts washed through Lizzy's spin-cycle, Charley made yet another confession. "I was married," he said, watching Lizzy's eyes judiciously. "Her name was Dani."

Charley began working as a copy editor for the *San Francisco Star* in the fall of 1985. Fresh out of college, it was his first *real* job. Before that, his resume amounted to nothing but wasted talent–or at least that's what his parents kept telling him. He'd spent five years mostly foundering in college, changing majors like he was choosing between a red tie and a yellow tie. When he graduated, with a degree in journalism, he had no real idea of what he wanted to do with his life.

Taking the job at the *Star* was a chance for him to prove himself, to show that his life had some direction–and to show that the hundred-grand investment his parents had made in him was worth more than Florida swampland. He even came in with lofty ambitions and high ideals, but working the overnight shift, being constantly berated by a fickle blowhard of an editor and repeatedly passed up for promotions, all the while earning barely enough to pay the rent, made him feel like he was in the shit-removal business.

That all changed when he met Dani. At the time, he knew her only by her byline–Danielle Christian. She was the paper's ace crime beat reporter, a star on the rise. Having just authored her first novel, *Don't Call Me Frisco*, a fictional crime story set in San Francisco's Mission District, a critically acclaimed local best seller, she was becoming the talk of the town–and the paper duly rewarded her, giving her a weekly column and a hefty pay raise. All of the notoriety didn't sit well with others in the newsroom, who had started to treat her like an unwelcome stepsister.

Working the overnight shift, Charley was segregated from most of the ugliness of office politics. Still, enough gossip leaked its way to him that he'd formed a generally unfavorable opinion of Miss Danielle Christian–even though he'd never seen her in the flesh. So it was with great surprise when one evening, around 10:30, working in solitude, he was interrupted by the intoxicating smell of French perfume.

"Are you Charley Hubbs?"

Glancing up from his computer screen, Charley was dumbstruck by beauty. Silky straight blond hair, tied in a ponytail, hung over her right shoulder. Azure eyes sparkled against her bronzed, smooth skin.

"Uh … yeah," he stuttered, wishing he didn't sound like a moronic caveman and wondering why his jaw seemed to be stuck in the open position.

"I was told you were hiding back here. I'm Dani, er Danielle–Danielle Christian." Charley didn't connect the name to the byline. "I think you've been editing my stories. I just wanted to thank you."

"Oh ... yes." Charley felt like he was still a beat behind. *"Thank you?"*

"Yes, I wanted to thank you for the fine job that you've been doing on editing my stories."

Charley paused to consider the compliment. "But I've never really done *anything* with your stories. I don't think I've done more than make a couple of spelling corrections."

"Yes, exactly. That's the way I like it." She raised her brows and crossed her arms as she looked down at Charley. "I put a lot of sweat into writing those stories. The last thing I need is to see them mangled by someone who has invested nothing into them and just decides, 'Oh, I've got a better way to write this.' I mean, what kind of an ego do you have to have to think you know a better way to do something than the person who's done all the research and interviews?"

Is she waiting for a response? Charley looked to her helplessly before he uttered, "A pretty big one, I suppose."

"Yes, exactly," she said, nodding. "A pretty big one."

Charley smiled. "You take reporting pretty seriously, I take it."

"You bet I do. Reporting's my life. It runs in my blood. My father was a journalist and so was his father. That makes me a third-generation journalist."

Charley looked at her with awe, wondering how she could be so sure of herself. "Did you go into journalism because your father wanted you to go into it?"

"No, I went into journalism because *I* wanted to be a journalist," she fired back. "If my father had his way, I'd be a doctor or a lawyer–or worse yet, pregnant and married to some rich business tycoon." She chuckled at the thought. "But I always knew this was what I wanted to be."

"You're lucky–knowing what you want to be. I still don't know what I want to be." That was the truth. He'd been pondering the idea for a couple weeks of surrendering and becoming a beach bum.

She looked at him curiously, really noticing him for the first time. "You don't know what you want to be?"

Charley shook his head and turned his palms to the sky. "No ... I guess I don't. Maybe you can help me."

"Well, if you want to be a reporter, I can help you. That's the only thing I know. Can you write?"

Charley paused to consider the question. "Yeah … or at least I think so."

"A better question. Do you *like* to write?"

"Yeah … yeah. I guess I do."

"No! None of this guessing stuff!" she huffed. "Do you like it, or don't you? There's no in-between."

Charley was taken in by her beauty, but was won over by her passion. She had in her something he always craved, and she helped him to become what he never thought he could be–somebody who cared about what he was doing. He grew to love reporting as he grew to love her. They were two pieces of a puzzle. They fit together. They belonged together.

A year later they were married. With Dani's guidance, encouragement and influence, Charley finally got his break. He became a big city courts reporter. Over time he became a good one, winning statewide awards. At times they teamed up–and it was like they were one. They were happy. But in a split second that all came to an end on a dark stretch of road north of San Francisco.

"Approximately two months before I found my way to Chicago," Charley explained to Lizzy, "there was an accident. I don't know exactly what happened. We–Dani and I–we'd been to a party. It was hosted by the publisher of the *Star*. His name is Joseph Kingman. He's a very powerful man. Maybe you've heard of him." He glanced at Lizzy but didn't wait for her to respond.

"The party was at this incredible mansion he has which overlooks the Pacific. It was a big deal. It was a big night for Dani especially. The party was really in her honor. She was coming out with a new book, or at least she was supposed to be. Nobody even knew what it was about. Not even me."

Lizzy looked at Charley curiously. "Your wife was writing a book, and you don't even know what it was about?"

Charley shook his head. "No, she was very secretive. Initially, I asked her about it, but she would just smile and say, 'You'll have to wait, just like everybody else.'" After that I left her alone. I figured if she wanted to talk about it, she would. But she never did."

"Weren't you curious?"

"Of course I was. I was dying to know what she was writing about. But at the same time, I respected her privacy. I respected her. I don't exactly know how to explain this … but Dani … she went into this other place at times when she was working. It was like she was off in another world. You didn't disturb her when she was there."

"But she must have dropped some kind of hints of what the book was about."

"Not really. The only thing she said was that it was fiction but that it was, in her words, 'based on truth,' and she said it would 'shake up San Francisco like the earthquake did four years ago.' Mr. Kingman, the publisher of the *Star*, was so feverish for it he was ready to run front-page excerpts of the book–without even knowing what it was about. That's what this party was all about. It was basically a coming-out party for Dani, and I must say she basked in the adulation. She had this glow about her that night." Charley paused as he remembered.

"She wore this beautiful blue gown that perfectly matched her eyes. She was a star–a bright and shining star. You could see it in her eyes–and in the way she moved. She, literally, stopped people in their tracks that evening. I watched her with pride. It was her night and she deserved it.

"But something happened about two hours into the party. I'm watching her. She's making her way around the room. She's got this permanent smile on her face and then … and then she comes to this gentleman and the smile fades. He's talking to her. She's not talking to him. Her face has turned ghost-white, and then she breaks away and comes for me. She's literally trembling. She says she wants to leave. I say okay. So we leave. We don't even say our good-byes. We're driving home and she's still obviously shaken. I ask her what's wrong. She says she can't talk about it. She just wants to go home. So there's this quiet between us that's so thick you can feel it. You know what I mean?"

Lizzy nodded. "I think I do."

"Anyway, I'm driving on a typically foggy Bay Area night. We're on this dark stretch of road lined with giant redwoods just a couple miles from the Highway 101 interchange when she suddenly cries out, 'Stop!' and grabs the steering wheel, like she sees something in the middle of the road. But there's nothing. The car swerves off the road and smashes into a tree. When I came to–I don't know how long I was out, maybe a couple seconds, maybe a couple minutes–blood's coming from my forehead. I'm groggy when I look over at Dani and I could tell right then ... she wasn't going to make it. The collision..." Charley paused as he fought back tears. "I still don't know what happened to her ... what caused her to do what she did ... I loved her so much."

Lizzy wiped the tears that fell from her eyes.

Charley pulled her into his arms and held her. He felt like a six hundred-pound gorilla had been lifted from his shoulders.

Lizzy pulled her head away and looked into Charley's eyes, feeling like she was seeing him for the first time.

"So you're *not* gay?" She smiled warmly as she wiped more tears from her eyes.

Charley's head jumped back. "You *thought* I was *gay?*"

"You did say no to this." She stepped back and, with her hands, swept over her body. "I mean, really, what was I to think?"

Charley chuckled. For the first time in a long time, he felt good. Yet he knew his troubles were miles away from over.

He now turned serious. "So you'll help me?"

The smile evaporated from Lizzy's face and her eyes zoomed in on Charley's. She reached out with her right hand and touched his face, slowly running her fingers down his unshaven cheeks until she put her index finger to his lips and moved her head closer. "Yes," she breathed. She tilted her head and put her lips to his.

Charley closed his eyes, losing himself in her lips. His body trembled as he gave into her. Pulling her tightly in, he lifted her off her feet. She was his, and he wasn't going to let his fears drive her away again.

Lying on her side, resting her body on her left elbow, Lizzy studied him. So peaceful, he appeared. Yet she knew he was anything but. To say the least, he was a complex figure–one who filled her with questions and doubts. Funny thing was, she liked that about him. He was everything that every other man wasn't. He was, to her, a mystery.

As if he could feel her eyes on him, Charley awoke from his slumber.

"Hi," Lizzy said, smiling. She stroked his thick hair.

"Hi. Have you been watching me long?"

"Long enough. Does that bother you?"

"No." Charley smiled warmly.

"So ... no regrets?" She'd never asked that question before of a man, but felt a need to do so this time—even if the answer hurt her.

"None. You?"

Lizzy closed her eyes for a moment. A smile crept on her face. "Maybe one regret."

Worry overcame Charley. Would she try to pull away from him?

"I didn't get to use my handcuffs on you," she said, smirking, as she lifted her brows.

"You'd use handcuffs on me?" Charley smiled.

"You are a fugitive after all, and I always get my man."

Chapter 13

Red Flags

Charley had one big secret left–the one he couldn't tell Lizzy yet. How could he tell her he had no idea how he'd ended up in Chicago? How could he explain two months of his life that he couldn't explain himself?

The only thing that he could tell her was that he had to go back to his apartment. She told him that was crazy, that he'd be pulling the go-back-to-jail card, and he knew she could be right. Yet he had no other choice. He had to find the key to unlock the mystery of two missing months, and he had a hunch that key was in his apartment.

The two detectives, Bone and O'Halloran, waited for Charley in a beat up old Dodge Dart, outside the Bradley Place Apartments, wired on 7-11 coffee.

"I'll tell ya," O'Halloran said, "Brandmeier wouldn't even be on the radio if it weren't for Dahl."

"Dat may be, my friend. But all'z I'm sayin' is dat right now, Brandmeier is da king of Chicago radio."

While the detectives debated Chicago radio personalities, Charley ducked into the short stairwell on the building's west side, which led down to the property manager's office. He peered through a window. There were no lights on. When he turned the doorknob, he found fortune on his side. The door was unlocked.

As he opened the door with a cautious hand, he heard snoring. Turning his head toward the couch, his eyes were able to make out the dark profile of a body wrapped in a blanket. Creeping closer, he saw that the sleeping stranger was Toby. With no time to wonder what Toby was doing there, he tiptoed on and found the door that led to the basement. From there, he made his way through the basement and up a flight of stairs, to the back door of his apartment. His luck was holding out. Exhaling, he inserted the key into his apartment and cautiously opened the door. The coast was clear. He sneaked inside, closing the door behind him.

After pausing to catch his breath, he tiptoed on through the kitchen and into the main room. There, he got an eyeful. The apartment had been ransacked–all of his papers and belongings littered the floor. Who would have done such a thing? Surely the cops had searched his apartment, but he couldn't believe they would do this. No, this was a reckless job. Somebody was in a hurry and was looking for something. *Was it the same thing he'd come for?*

His eyes scanned the floor but didn't see the one thing they were searching for. He traipsed through the clutter and came to the closet. His suitcases had been taken out and contents strewn about the floor. The shoes on the floor of the closet had been kicked around. The hangers holding his shirts and coats had been shoved to the sides but remained perched on the bar. There, he saw it. The long gray wool coat was pressed against the side of the closet. The coat had been an early anniversary gift from Dani. She'd bought it for him in anticipation of a trip to Paris. They never made it there, and he'd never worn the coat. He kept it only because he couldn't bear to part with it.

He ripped the coat off its hanger, felt the left sleeve, and breathed a sigh of relief. Reaching into the sleeve, he pulled out a large manila envelope. As he did so, he heard a key being inserted into the lock of the front door. The time had come for him to leave, so he dropped the coat, clutched the envelope in his hand and scampered out the back door.

As a means of escape from his partner, Detective Bone had wandered out of the patrol car and up to the apartment. When he opened the door, he stopped cold in his tracks. The apartment had been clean only an hour ago. Now it looked like a tornado had swept through. He pulled out his walkie-talkie. "We've got a problem here."

O'Halloran's bushy eyebrows turned up. "I'll be right up."

When he arrived at the front door to the apartment, O'Halloran's eyes couldn't believe what they saw. "What the–"

"Yeah, I know," Bone said soberly.

"Whatchya think happened? You think he's been back?"

"Yeah he's been back. I can smell his stinkin' hide in here."

"The shit's gonna hit the fan if they get wind of this up at the precinct."

Bone fired a warning shot with his eyes. A year ago he'd lost his longtime partner, Russell "Rusty" Gunn, in an undercover drug deal gone bad. When he returned to the force after a month away on paid administrative leave, he asked to work alone. Instead, he got O'Halloran, a rookie detective from Downtown with a squeaky-clean reputation. Bone knew O'Halloran was raw and just needed a little seasoning from a veteran. "That ain't gonna happen, 'cause they ain't gonna find out," Bone said.

When it came to men, Lizzy knew the typical red flags. There were the last-minute date cancellations. The unexplained phone calls. Sometimes, there was a tan line on the ring finger. Other times, there was a hint of perfume on the collar.

Charley was draped in a red flag. So why wasn't she running from him? She pondered that question as she entered through the doors to the library at DePaul University. For two years, she'd studied philosophy there. She'd been an honors student there, but dropped out after one of her professors with whom she'd started a relationship broke it off, telling her he was married. This was her first time back on the campus in four years.

She wanted to believe in Charley. Her fear was that she was falling in love with him or, worse yet, had already taken the plunge. But there were doubts that she couldn't shake–pieces of his story that just didn't add up. So there she was in the library searching for answers on a microfiche reader.

After almost two hours, the beginnings of an answer came to her weary eyes. There it was, in black and white, on the front page of the July 14, 1993 edition of the *San Francisco Star*, under the byline of James Mason. The main headline–MYSTERY SURROUNDS REPORTER'S DEATH–intrigued her. But the sub-heading–HUSBAND MISSING AFTER FATAL CRASH–really caught her eye. *Husband missing?*

Her interest piqued, she read on. The story told of the car crash that killed

Dani, just as Charley had described–but what Charley had left out was the mystery of his own disappearance after the crash. According to the story, local police were baffled and didn't know if Charley had been injured, wandered off or fled.

Lizzy scratched her head. What did it all mean? She scanned through the microfiche until she came to a follow-up story, also written by Mason, dated two days later under the headline, REPORTER STILL MISSING; POLICE HAVE NO LEADS.

Lizzy sat frozen, her eyes blurry from staring at the words so long. She tried to make sense of it all but nothing seemed to add up. Why would Charley have just walked away? Why hadn't he told her all of this? Sure there was the possibility he just couldn't deal with his wife's death. Maybe he just ran away. But what if his reason for running was more sinister than that? What if he'd killed his wife–and now had killed two more people? She trembled at the thought.

Without bothering to put away the microfiche, she raced down the stairs to the front desk. A librarian there pointed her to the pay phones, which were next to the bathrooms, around the corner. Breathlessly, Lizzy thanked the librarian and then made her way to the pay phones. Once there, she hurriedly dialed directory assistance and asked to be put through to the newsroom at the *San Francisco Star*. She scoured through her purse for every quarter she could find and dumped them all into the coin slot. When the phone picked up on the other end, Lizzy was breathing heavily. "May I speak … with James Mason, please," she said. "Please be there. Please be there," she chanted under her breath.

"*Star*. This is Mason."

"Oh, thank you," Lizzy said breathlessly.

"May I help you?"

Lizzy exhaled as she tried to calm herself. "Yes, you're Mr. James Mason?"

"Yes, why?"

"You wrote a couple of stories a few months ago about Charley Hubbs' disappearance after his wife's death in a car crash."

"Yes. Yes, I did." Mason sat up in his chair. A story about Charley's courtroom escape had just come over the wires. He reached with his right hand for a pen and flipped open his notebook. "Who's this?"

"I can't tell you that. I just need to know one thing."

"Yes?"

"Has there been any other news about Charley since his disappearance?"

Mason made a quick adjustment in his chair. "No, no there hasn't. Not until this news that just came over the wire earlier today about his escape. I was wondering whether this was our Charley boy. Your phone call makes me pretty sure that it is. I take it you know something."

"Yes. No. Maybe. I can't talk to you right now."

She hung up the phone, leaving Mason hanging on the other end. When she turned around, she was startled by the presence of a tall man with a scraggly beard.

"I think we need to talk," the man said.

The face looked familiar but she couldn't place it. "Do I know you?"

"Not exactly. I've been in your bar before, but we've never been formally introduced. My name is Grandstroke. Dr. Thomas Grandstroke."

She remembered now. "You're the notebook guy?"

"So you do recognize me." He smiled.

"Yes. You've been in a couple times. You're always scribbling into that notebook. I'm sorry, you said your name is *Grandstroke*?" *Why did that name ring a bell?* Moments later, she remembered–Charley's dream.

"Dr. Grandstroke," he corrected. "I was Charley's doctor."

Confused, Lizzy shook her head. "Charley's doctor?"

"Yes, I treated him after the accident. I'm a neuro-psychiatrist."

"But I don't understand. I read the stories in the newspaper. Charley disappeared. You mean to tell me he didn't?"

"Nobody just disappears. He was sick, and I helped him."

"What do you mean?"

"I think we'd better sit down for this. Come with me."

The doctor led Lizzy to a private study room on the library's second floor. There, he told Lizzy that he was a friend of Charley's wife, Dani, and that they had been working on a book together, which was due for release soon. "Charley didn't know this was a collaborative effort until the night of the party at Joseph Kingman's mansion. When he saw Dani and me talking, well, I think he got the wrong idea about our relationship."

155

Grandstroke claimed that Charley and Dani argued at the party. "It was quite obvious Charley had had too much to drink. He pulled Dani away from me. Let me just say, he made quite the scene. He was obviously very angry and very drunk. I watched them get into the car together and I thought to myself, this could be trouble.

"So I followed them. I was the first one to arrive at the crash site. I found Dani in the car, but Charley was gone. I called the police and reported that there had been an accident, and that was the end of it ... until the next morning when I showed up at my office and there was Charley sitting at my desk. Somehow he'd gotten in. Anyway, I was obviously startled. I didn't know what to expect. He looked like he'd been through a war. His face was still covered in dried blood. He had cuts and abrasions all over. His clothes were tattered. And he didn't speak. He just sat there, numb, almost like he was in a catatonic state.

"I took care of him. I cleaned him up. Bandaged his wounds. Then I began to try to heal him mentally. I called my secretary, told her I had an emergency and to cancel my appointments. Then I took Charley home with me."

Lizzy looked at the doctor curiously. "I don't understand. Why didn't you call the police? Why were you helping him?"

Grandstroke nodded, as if he'd anticipated the questions. "I knew from seeing him that he was very sick, mentally if not physically as well. I knew he needed medical care. I knew I could give it to him, and I knew he wouldn't get the kind of help he needed if I called the police. Plus, remember, I was a good friend of his wife. In some ways, I did this for her. I thought it would be what she would want."

Lizzy shook her head, confused. "What do you mean by saying that he was *sick*?"

"He had all the signs of post-traumatic stress syndrome, often referred to as shell-shock or battle fatigue. Basically, his mind couldn't accept what he'd been through. It was like he'd been through war and seen unspeakable horrors of battle. His mind deals with that by blanking it out. In his mind, it is like the horrible event didn't happen."

"That's not true," Lizzy shot back. "He told me what happened."

"And I suppose he blamed his wife for causing the accident and not himself," the doctor shot back with a raise of his right brow. Lizzy closed her eyes and nodded, feeling like her heart had been ripped from her. "I spent almost two months with him. I know him, and I know he's still very sick. I followed his trail here after he one day got up and walked away."

Lizzy was trembling, her teeth chattering. "You think he killed these people, don't you?"

Grandstroke returned a solemn nod. "I told you he is very sick. I never should have allowed him to get away," he said with a bitter aftertaste. "I never..."

Lizzy drilled into the doctor's eyes. "What do you want from *me*?"

"I want you to convince him to turn himself in. It's the only way."

Chapter 14
Crazy Sense

Steam breathed out of Charley's mouth, as he rested his head against the red brick of Lizzy's apartment building. In his tingling, nearly numb hands, he clutched the manila envelope.

Scrawled on the outside of the envelope, in black marker, was the word MANUSCRIPT. While unpacking soon after he'd moved into Bradley Place, he'd stumbled upon it. How it had gotten there he had no idea. As far as he knew, he'd never laid eyes on it before. Still, when he saw it he knew what it was, and he couldn't bear to read it. Doing so would bring back memories he'd been trying to escape from. So he tucked it into the sleeve of the coat he knew he'd never wear.

Now, as he shivered with curled lips and watery eyes, holding the envelope tightly against his chest, he prayed for the first time since Dani's death. "Please Lord, I know I'm not a perfect man. I'm not much of a praying man, either. But I'm at my rope's end here, and I need your help. So, please, please tell me I did not do these horrendous things of which I've been accused. Lead me in the right direction. Oh, Lord … help me."

Lizzy paced inside her apartment, not knowing whether she should be angry with him, sad for him, or afraid of him. Worst of all, she didn't know what she would tell him.

The doorbell startled her. "Get yourself together," she mumbled to herself. She composed herself by closing her eyes and taking a deep breath. When she felt she was ready, she buzzed him up.

As he bounced up the stairs, she bit on a fingernail. When he reached the top stair and stepped forward to kiss her, she turned away.

"What is it?" Charley asked.

Feeling the heat of his body next to hers made her tremble. Seeing his searching eyes made her ache. "Nothing," she said, unconvincingly. "Come on in."

As she trailed, she glimpsed the manila envelope but gave it no more than a passing thought. Her very being was torn apart. She couldn't believe–didn't want to believe–that the man she slept with–the man she might love–was a killer.

But it all added up–everything the doctor had said made perfect sense. Charley was sick. He needed help. And she couldn't be selfish.

They sat silently on the couch. Occasionally eyes met but then darted away.

"What's this?" She put the fingers of her left hand on the envelope, which he clung to tightly.

Charley breathed a sigh of relief. He assumed the awkwardness between them was because they'd slept together, which he didn't regret at all. What he did regret was his bone-headed decision to flee so abruptly afterwards, without explaining why. He could see why she'd be angry–or at the very least have doubts about him, but now he had an opportunity to explain himself–and, hopefully, ease her mind.

"This is why I left this morning," he explained. "This is a manuscript."

"A manuscript?"

"Yes. It was *hers*." He eyed her intently, wanting to make certain she understood.

"You mean…"

"Yes, this was the book she was working on."

"I don't understand," she said, shaking her head. "You said you hadn't read it."

"I haven't."

"But you've had it all this time? Charley, I don't get it."

"I don't, either." Charley went on to explain what he didn't understand himself, telling her how he'd found the manuscript and how he'd gone back to retrieve it.

"I think in the accident I suffered a head injury that might explain why I don't remember certain things and why I have these blackout spells. I've done some research on these kinds of things. It's not all that uncommon to have epileptic-type seizures after sustaining a blow to the head, and it's also not all that uncommon to have some kind of amnesia after such an accident. What confused me is why I remember everything before the accident but couldn't remember much of what happened after the accident. But there's this amnesia, called anterograde amnesia, which makes it difficult to remember ongoing events after suffering a head injury. You don't lose any memory of your past, but you have trouble holding short-term memories. The thing is, this kind of amnesia is rarely permanent. From what I've read, in most cases people recover within two or three months. That explains why I remember things now that I don't remember during the first two months after the accident."

Charley was almost breathless as his eyes darted about. "Don't you see, Lizzy, this all makes some kind of crazy sense."

Lizzy did see, with more clarity than she wanted. She saw what she'd hoped she wouldn't see. "You're sick, Charley." Her eyes welled with tears.

"No, you're ... you're not understanding what I'm telling you. I *was* sick. I'm better now."

With her hands over her eyes, Lizzy dropped her head, unable to hold back the tears. As Charley reached for her, she pulled away.

"My God, Charley," she said through the tears, "I saw him today."

"Saw who?"

"The doctor ... Doctor Grandstroke."

Charley looked at Lizzy as if he was seeing her for the first time. "That's the name from my dream, Lizzy. He doesn't really exist."

"Oh, my God, Charley, you really don't remember?"

"Remember what?"

"He cared for you ... after the accident."

"You're kidding, right?"

"No, Charley, I'm not," Lizzy said, wiping tears from her eyes with her hands. "You're very sick. And I think...I think you need to turn yourself in."

Charley's jaw dropped as he realized what she was telling him. "You think I killed those people. *Don't* you?"

"Charley, you need help." Tears now washed down her face.

"Liz…" Charley reached out one more time, desperation pouring from his veins, but again she pulled away. "I didn't do these things, Lizzy."

But Charley saw the one thing he hoped he'd never see. He saw that he'd lost her. There was only one option left. He'd have to go it alone. As tears welled in his eyes, he stormed out the door.

"Charley," she bawled, as she watched him stamp down the stairs. "Oh, Charley…" She collapsed to the floor in a flood of tears.

Chapter 15
Damn De Luck

Numb to the cold, Charley ran. A kaleidoscope of thoughts and images whirled through his head. He was on a runaway carnival ride, spinning out of control. Going east on Waveland, he shot past the north side of Wrigley Field, then past the alleyway where Leah's body had been dumped, until he came to a stop at Halsted. One block south was the 23rd District Chicago police station. For a moment, he thought of turning himself in, but instead he dashed across Halsted. Oblivious to the traffic, he narrowly avoided getting hit by a car. At the next block, Broadway, he turned south. Tears trickling from his eyes clouded his vision so he didn't see the vendor on the street hawking *Streetwise*, a newspaper for the homeless.

Devon went down like a bowling pin. Splayed out on his back, with Charley sprawled over his tall, slender frame, Devon felt like a Mack truck had hit him. Lifting his head a bit from the concrete, a twinge of pain shot from his neck to his head. Through the stars in his eyes, he glimpsed the thick, dark hair on Charley's head resting on his chest. Pulling up his right arm from the ground, he nudged Charley in the side.

"Hey, you," Devon uttered. When that didn't work, he cleared his throat in an effort to get Charley's attention.

Charley cautiously opened his eyes, blinking a few times as he tried to clear the fog. As his eyes adjusted, they identified an arm that wasn't this own.

Inching his head up, he glimpsed yellow hair framing smooth, dark black skin.

"Hey, I know you," Devon said.

Charley sprung to his feet and put out his right hand to Devon. "Are you okay?"

"Yeah, I dink so," Devon said, as he grabbed Charley's hand. "Mah neck and head hurt a liddle, but I dink I'll be awright, mahn."

Charley pulled up Devon. As Devon brushed off his clothes, Charley saw blood trickling out of the back of his head, staining his yellow hair. "Your head's bleeding."

Devon felt the abrasion on the back of his head, then saw the blood residue on his right hand. "I guess I am. I didn't even realize–"

"You need to get to a hospital. You could have a concussion."

Devon laughed uncomfortably. "No, I doan dink so. Devon and hospitals doan mix well, mahn." Touching the abrasion again, he squinted in pain. "No, I'll be awright, mahn. Nudding dat a Band-Aid and a stiff drink cahn't fix."

Turning his focus to Charley, Devon said, "You doan remember me, do you, mahn?"

Charley shook his head. "Should I remember you?"

"I was *dare* dat night." Devon studied Charley's eyes, searching for a sign of recognition.

"You were *where*? I don't understand."

"Dat night at de bar, when you decked dat dude. I was dare."

Thinking he knew what was coming, Charley closed his eyes and put his right hand to his forehead. "Look, if you want to turn me in, go ahead. I really don't care anymore."

Devon realized Charley was misconstruing his words. "Chill, mahn. I know you didn't kill dat dude."

"What did you just say?"

"Yah, mahn. I saw everyding. Dat dude you decked … he's not the dude dat's dead."

Charley's ears lit up. "How do you know this? You witnessed the murder?"

"Nah, mahn. Devon's eyes didn't see dat ugliness, but day sure saw de ugliness after. Dat mahn in de batroom was not de mahn you gave it to."

"What do you mean?"

"De mahn you hit, he was in drag. De mahn in de batroom, he wasn't wearin' no makeup. Day was two different dudes."

"And you're absolutely sure of this?"

"Sure as ahm standin' here wit mah head bleedin', mahn."

"And you could testify to this?" Charley excitedly grabbed Devon's lanky arms.

"Woh, mahn! Devon and de courts, day doan get along."

Charley stepped back. He put his fingertips to his temples. "I got it. Just give me a phone number. I think I can keep your name out of this. You'll just have to tell what you told me to the editor of my newspaper."

Devon looked to the ground as he scratched his head. "I doan have a phone."

"You don't have a phone?"

Devon shook his head. "I'm homeless. Dat's why I'm selling dem." He motioned toward the *Streetwise* newspapers, which were strewn about the ground.

Charley nodded. "Do you have a place I can find you then?"

Devon considered the question for a moment. "De Coronado Hotel on Belmont. You cahn find me dare."

Charley took Devon's right hand, clasped it in his own and wrapped his left hand around it. "Thank you. I mean that. You've given me hope."

Gazing into Charley's eyes, Devon smiled bashfully. "Dare's no chahns for us, is dare?"

Charley shook his head. "I'm already in love with somebody," he confessed, not just to Devon, but to himself as well.

"Damn de luck," Devon said, dispiritedly. "Damn de luck."

As Charley started to walk away, Devon called out to him. "You forgot sometin!"

Charley turned and saw Devon standing there, looking like a cross between Jimmie Walker and Dennis Rodman. In his hands was the manila envelope.

"You must have dropped it when you fell into me."

"You're a good guy, Devon."

Devon eyed Charley like he'd heard that line hundreds of times before. "Dat's mah curse, mahn. Dat's mah curse."

At Addison, a walkway runs underneath busy Lake Shore Drive, a convenient connection to the shores of Lake Michigan for pedestrians and bicyclists. For Charley, the darkly lit underground walkway now served as his protection against Chicago's infamous whipping winds and as his hiding place.

Sitting with his back resting against the graffiti-blemished concrete wall, amid the stench of urine, Charley blew into his cupped hands, trying to warm himself. Time was running out. Devon had given him hope, but he needed more. He needed proof, and his search for proof had him digging up words from the grave.

For several moments, he did nothing but stare at the manila envelope, which rested against his bent legs. Then he took a deep breath and tore into the envelope. Inside there was an inch-thick manuscript. On the first page was typed PROVISIONAL DIAGNOSIS: MURDER.

Charley turned the page. Chapter one began in morbidly chilling fashion. It read, "This book could not be written if I were alive. That is why I killed myself."

Charley knew Dani had a flair for the dramatic, but this was downright eerie. Could it be that the book was her suicide note? Or was this some misguided attempt at achieving writing immortality?

As he read on, Charley got a different picture. Dani told of how she'd changed her name, donned a brunette wig and went undercover to investigate a possible serial killer, a neuropsychiatrist named Thomas Grandstroke.

That name again. First it came to him in a dream. Then it came from Lizzy. And now it came from the dead. There was some kind of connection, but what was it? How had Dani come to know him? Was he real? Or was he a fictional creation, a product of Dani's vivid imagination? A spicy mixture of thoughts stirred through Charley's mind, causing his stomach to do somersaults.

As he skimmed through the pages over the next three hours, Charley came to believe that Grandstroke was not a fictional character. Perhaps Dani had changed his name for literary purposes, but Charley was almost certain that he existed–and that Dani knew him, inside and out. The story read as too real for fiction. Dani had put herself into the story as if she'd lived it–and if she had, she made it seem like she'd met the devil incarnate.

In two hundred and fifty pages, Dani had portrayed a man devoid of conscience, a diabolical doctor who had used his position as a means to murder. The book documented six mental patients who had died under Grandstroke's care between 1985 and 1991. In each case the medical examiner had determined the cause of death to be suicide.

To Dani's eyes, there was something strange going on. The sister of one of the deceased had come to her in early 1992, asking for help. She told Dani how she believed her sister, who was bipolar, wasn't suicidal, but the police dismissed her pleas. Dani agreed to look into it, not expecting it to amount to anything. Mostly she felt sorry for the sister. Then she uncovered five other presumed suicides, all patients of Grandstroke.

Starting in 1985, Dani outlined one suicide for each successive year through 1991. They were all young women in their twenties or early thirties– and all died by different means. The deaths, in order of occurrence, were by drug overdose, motor vehicle exhaust poisoning, hanging, jumping, wrist slashing, and drowning. The one common thread was that none of the alleged suicide victims had written a suicide note.

In the end, Dani couldn't prove Grandstroke was a killer. The autopsies were all conclusive for suicide, the bodies buried. She even put herself at risk, going undercover, pretending to be suffering from depression. She donned the wig and changed her name to Alisa Abbott, her mother's maiden name. Over the course of two months, she saw Grandstroke on a weekly basis. In blunt detail, she described the sessions and how, over time, he seemed to become increasingly amorous towards her. But that was all.

The last words Lizzy wrote were–"Six women. All dead. Did they kill themselves? Or were they victims of a mad doctor? The answer may never be known ... unless one day I too am found dead in an apparent suicide. And, God forbid if that should happen. Just be sure of one thing. It wasn't what you think."

A chill ran though Charley's spine as he turned the final page. He looked down again at the title page. Was it possible? Could Dani have been murdered, and, if so, how? The whole thing seemed so crazy that it might just be true.

Chapter 16

The Deadline

Lizzy eased her eyes open to the blackness of the trunk of a rented Cadillac sedan speeding southbound on the Dan Ryan Expressway. When the car hit a series of potholes, she winced as her head, already reeling from headache, banged against the trunk floor. She felt like she was riding home on the "L" train after an all-night party.

The fog in her head had cleared just enough so that she knew only one thing for sure. She was in quite a pickle. Being locked in the trunk of a moving car was bad enough, but, to make matters worse, her wrists were bound together behind her back, her ankles were tied together, and her head felt like it had taken a beating from a baseball bat.

Unable to escape, she did the first thing that came to her mind. She kicked the trunk door with her feet and let out an expletive-laden cry for help. Her desperate cries went unheard—even by the driver of the rented Cadillac sedan.

Henry was fifteen minutes late for his shift that night at the Ginger Man. This was unusual for him. He didn't like it when other bartenders showed up late for their shifts, so he tried not to be late for his. On most days, he was a good fifteen minutes early. Today, he'd lost track of time while rearranging his CD collection and gotten into a fender-bender as he rushed to get to the bar. He was shaking his head and putting together an apology while sorting through his cache of keys for the bar's back door when he noticed something unusual. The door was ajar. For a couple of moments, he stared at the door, a puzzled look on his face. This just wasn't like Lizzy. The bar owner was very strict about one thing, and one thing only. The back door was always to be shut tight. Lizzy was too responsible to have not made sure the door was closed when she came in. Had the owner himself stopped by for a second, and, in a rush, left the door ajar? Henry cast aside that notion. He'd have noticed the owner's red Camaro around the corner. With a shrug of his shoulders, he walked inside, first making sure to close the door behind him.

As he started to pull the backpack off his shoulder, Henry glimpsed a burly redheaded male straddled up to the bar grasping a pint. The bar was otherwise empty. Lizzy was nowhere to be seen, but he didn't think much of it, figuring she was either in the bathroom or downstairs, in the stockroom. After making his way around to the bar, he dropped his backpack on the floor. A nod to the lone customer was met by a grunt. This, too, he shrugged off and went about his routine, making sure that the fridge was stocked with beer and that the ice bin was full. After wiping the counter, he noticed that his only customer's pint was empty. "Can I get you a refill, bud?"

"On the house?" the customer replied with a wry smile.

Henry grabbed the glass and winked. "Sure, bud. Another Guinness?"

The customer grunted, then glanced over his shoulder, looking in the direction of the entry door.

"You waiting for somebody?" Henry asked.

The customer turned and looked at Henry as if he'd forgotten he was even there. "Wazaat?" he growled.

"It looked like … ah, never mind." Henry slid the pint over to the customer. As he was about to turn away, he scratched his head. "Say, you wouldn't happen to know where the bartender I'm relieving is, would you?"

The customer put down the pint, stared at it for a moment, then turned his head toward Henry. "The girl?"

Henry nodded. "Yeah, cute, dark-haired. I'm supposed to be relieving her."

"She had to leave unexpectedly, I'm afraid."

Something was rotten in Wrigleyville. Henry knew Lizzy well enough to know she would never have left the back door ajar *and* left the bar unattended. "What do you mean she had to leave *unexpectedly*?" He stood rigid and eyed the mysterious customer, clinging to a bar rag like it was a life preserver.

At that moment the front door burst open and Charley stormed in, breathing heavily. He came to an abrupt halt upon seeing his newsroom buddy, Piper.

"What the–" Charley coughed out.

Recognizing Charley from the mug shot that had been all over the news the last twenty-four hours, Henry now realized why the face had seemed so familiar to him. He was the guy Lizzy had left with a couple months back. Fearing that something dreadful had happened to Lizzy, he picked up the phone off the wall.

Piper was growing annoyed. "Put the phone down, son."

Henry obeyed, seeing the shiny black barrel of the Smith and Wesson .38 revolver pointing at him, looking like the snout on a Doberman.

"What the hell's goin' on here, Piper?" Charley kept his distance as he eyed the handgun.

"The only thing goin' on, kid, is you. You and me, we're goin' for a little ride."

While turning the revolver in Charley's direction, Piper stood and gulped his pint. He glanced at Henry, who looked like he was about to piss in his pants, if he hadn't already done so. Piper told Henry he'd live if he simply ripped the phone out of the wall.

Henry didn't know what to do. Piper made the decision easy for him by waving the gun in his face. "*Now!*" he barked.

Henry did as he was told. The phone came out of the wall and Henry went to the floor.

Piper now turned his attention to Charley. After drifting his way, he positioned the gun in the middle of his spine. "Let's go, kid. You've got an appointment and you're already late."

The rented Cadillac sedan came to an abrupt stop in a gravel parking lot outside the Covert Motel, a $29.95-a-night hellhole.

Before he'd broken in through a backdoor of the Ginger Man and taken Lizzy by surprise, Doctor Thomas Grandstroke had spent about six hours combing Chicago's South Side and south suburbs for a perfect hideaway. When he found the Covert Motel, he knew he'd found what he was looking for. Located just twenty miles outside Chicago's city limits, in an unincorporated part of Cook County, outside the town limits of Thornton–home to the world's largest limestone quarry–the seedy sleepover was the perfect hiding spot for people doing things they didn't want others to see–like kidnapping.

The Covert was far enough off the road that the few cars passing in the night couldn't see the dirty dealings taking place in its parking lot. Grandstroke had parked the sedan in front of Room 3B, at the west end of the motel. He'd gotten the room key when he first found the motel earlier that day after telling a nosy old lady behind the front desk that he planned to stay *indefinitely*. When she asked him what's his business, he answered curtly that it was none of hers and placed a crisp one hundred dollar bill on the desk in front of her. "No more questions," he instructed. The clerk grabbed the money as if it might evaporate if she didn't act soon enough. She didn't say a word afterward.

When he got out of the sedan and stepped into the still of the early evening moonlight, Grandstroke scoped the area as he ran the fingers of his right hand through his slicked back hair. The vacancy sign shone by the main road, but its light didn't cast on the parking lot, which was shrouded by trees and bushes and looked like a gravel graveyard, empty except for one other car belonging to the front desk clerk. A smile came to the doctor's face. This was just as he'd envisioned it. Reaching into the front pocket of his Versace dress slacks with his long, thin fingers, he pulled out the room key and trunk key. The fun was just beginning.

Lizzy's eyes took a couple of seconds to adjust in the darkness before she was able to make out the face of her abductor. As she was about to let out a scream, Grandstroke stuffed a rolled up handkerchief in her mouth. "Sorry. Necessary precaution, you understand."

As Lizzy squirmed, Grandstroke wrapped his arms around her and lifted her with some difficulty out of the trunk. When he had his balance, he carried her to the motel room, oblivious to her struggles. At the door, he turned his body to the side, reached a hand out from underneath her body, and inserted the room key into the lock. After a turn of the key, he nudged the door open with a shoulder. From there he moved to the center of the room and dropped Lizzy on the single queen-sized bed, draped in a flowery bedspread.

Lizzy was petrified but knew she had to retain her cool. She rocked herself into a sitting position and scooted to the end of the bed. Then she turned her gaze on Grandstroke, fire and fear raging in her eyes.

Grandstroke returned a casual smile. This was a moment to enjoy. With an air of supremacy, he crossed his arms across his chest. "So we meet again. I apologize that it has to be under such distasteful circumstances. I like you, Lizzy. I don't want to harm you, and I won't have to if you cooperate. Do you understand what I'm saying?"

Lizzy nodded, keeping her eyes focused on Grandstroke.

"Good. Well, the first issue is the handkerchief in your mouth. I'll remove it, but you must promise me that you'll not scream. First of all, I've got a strong aversion to loud noises. Secondly, it's highly unlikely that anyone would hear you anyway."

Grandstroke scratched his left ear as he looked away for a moment. "Besides, it would only force me to do something I really don't want to do. You understand, don't you?"

Lizzy nodded again.

"Good, I'm glad." He reached down with his right hand and was about to pull out the handkerchief when he had the impulse to stroke her right cheek. As his hand met her soft skin, he shivered with delight.

Lizzy bristled and turned her head in disgust.

"There-there, my dear," Grandstroke said, running his cold fingers through her hair. When his fingers reached the knot of the handkerchief, he put both arms around her and untied the knot.

Lizzy coughed and gazed up at her abductor with a scowl.

"That's better, now isn't it?"

Lizzy replied by spitting in her abductor's face.

The warm saliva against his cool skin elicited a pleasing sensation that grew in intensity as he guided it with his fingertips from his left cheek to his lips until he was able to coax it into his mouth with his tongue. Like a fine wine, he swished it around in his mouth and then swallowed. "You taste good, my dear."

Lizzy put her right hand to her forehead.

"You have a headache," the doctor diagnosed. "That's a natural side effect of the chloroform."

Lizzy's eyes penetrated Grandstroke like daggers.

"Yes, that's what I used to knock you out. I know, not that original, but it's effective nevertheless."

"What do you want from me?" Lizzy fired back, eyes burning.

"Ah, you speak. I'm so glad. What do I want from you?" He pondered the question for a moment. "That's a difficult question. I guess what I really want is for you to bring Charley to me."

"How am I supposed to do that?"

"Patience, my dear. Patience." With the tips of his fingers, he stroked her right cheek again. "Don't worry. He'll come."

The black 1990 Pontiac Firebird blended into the night. Behind the wheel, Piper kept his eyes on the road.

In the back seat, Charley sat, his hands bound behind his back with duct tape, trying to piece it all together in his mind. After holding it all in for fifteen minutes, he broke the silence. "Why'd you do it?" he asked.

Piper lifted his eyes and looked at Charley through the rear-view mirror. "Hah, he speaks."

Charley repeated his question.

Piper chuckled. "When did you first know?"

"That story about Jimmie's murder. There's no way you got it to press unless you already knew what was going to happen."

"Yeah, that was a good one, huh? Ol' Buzz was so wet over getting the scoop he didn't even stop to think how I got it in on deadline. *Deadline*– that really was a *dead*-line." Piper laughed heartily.

Charley interrupted Piper's laugher. "You didn't answer the question. *Why?*"

"Come on. Why wouldn't I? You're a reporter. You know how we work our ass off just to get shit on. My career was over years ago, kid. I've been stuck in that death hole–can you believe it–almost twenty-five years. And what do I have to show for it?" He eyed Charley in the rear-view again. "Fuckin' shit, that's what. Then one day this crazy fucker–and let me tell ya, this guy is one crazy fucker–he comes to me and offers me the story of a lifetime … and a shitload of money to boot. I paid my dues, kid. Now it's payday for ol' Piper."

A couple minutes later, the Firebird rolled into the gravel parking lot of the Covert Motel. Piper brought the car to a stop next to the Cadillac sedan and turned off the headlights. "This is the end of the road for you, kid. Sorry it has to end this way."

Charley eyed Piper, venom seeping from his eye ducts. "This story's not written yet, Piper."

"Yeah, it is, kid. Yeah, it is."

Piper exited the Firebird, leaving the motor running. With a motion of his head, he coaxed Charley out of the back seat. As Charley glared, Piper unwrapped the duct tape from his wrists. "Sorry it had to end this way, kid. Nothing personal. I actually kind of liked you. You've got some spunk. But this was a friendship that just wasn't meant to be."

Leaving Charley standing in the gravel, Piper got back in the Firebird. "Gotta deadline to make, kid."

As he looked out the car window at his former colleague, he chortled. *What a chump.* There had been a time when he'd have felt sorry for a poor, old dupe like that, but years of hardening by the news business had left him cold to the plight of others. Even the victims were beyond his compassion. Most of them were nothing more than faceless names on a crime report. Many of them were dead and buried. So why waste time caring about them? His job was to write about them, not care about them. The victims were a necessary evil. Without them, there wouldn't be a crime, and without a crime, there wouldn't be a story. The demands of the job were such that he had to move on, from one story to the next. There wasn't time for him to dwell on the pain, anguish or suffering of those he wrote about. No, the only person he cared about now was himself. That's why he was able to put the gas pedal to the floor and speed out of the parking lot, scattering gravel in his wake, without once looking back.

Grandstroke appraised Lizzy with hunger in his eyes. The taste of her saliva had whet his appetite. She looked good enough to eat, and might go well with a glass of French cabernet. "You know, your Charley's been a very bad boy." He wet his lips with his tongue.

"What do you mean by that?" Fire burned in Lizzy's eyes.

"I just mean, it wasn't supposed to have happened this way."

"Happen what way?"

"If your boyfriend had just played by the script, it would have all been so easy." Grandstroke pulled aside the curtain and looked out into the blackness of the night. A wicked smile came to his face when he saw Charley standing under the light of the motel vacancy sign.

"What do you mean … if Charley had *played* along?"

Grandstroke turned and looked at Lizzy as if the question had surprised him. "You know, I knew he'd go back to her. That's how I was able to follow him."

"Go back to whom?"

"To Dani, of course."

A puzzled look came to Lizzy's face. "Dani's dead. *Isn't she?*"

"Oh, yes, I made sure of that. The problem was Charley. I should have killed him then and there, but I wanted that damn book. That *damn* book … I thought he'd lead me to it." Again, he turned and pulled aside the curtains. "Don't worry, it will all be over soon enough."

"You killed them … didn't you?"

Grandstroke admitted his misdeeds benignly, like he'd just swatted a couple of flies. "Dirty business," he said, still gazing out the window. "A very dirty business, indeed."

Lizzy managed to pull a nail file out of her back jeans pocket and started to shave off the threads of the inch-thick rope that bound her wrists. As she filed away at the rope, her eyes trailed Grandstroke. He ambled across the room, picked up a briefcase and set it on the dresser. She watched him pull a small key out of his pants pocket, unlock the briefcase, and remove two vials and a case.

The case held two syringes and two needles. With Grandstroke's back turned toward her, Lizzy was unable to see him preparing the lethal injections. "Have you ever heard of succinylcholine, my dear?"

The sound of his voice startled Lizzy, causing her to freeze for a moment, but she was able to cough out, "No", before he turned his head. When he turned back to the syringes, Lizzy began again to pare away at the rope.

"It's an anesthetic." He spoke in a calm, clinical tone. "Fairly common. It's made of two compounds, succinic acid and choline, both of which are found naturally in the body. That makes it difficult to detect, which makes it a nearly ideal drug of choice if you're trying to get away with murder. Did you ever hear of the case of Doctor Carl Coppolino?"

This time Lizzy was better composed and answered with a quick, "No."

"In the 1960's," the doctor droned on, "Carl was convicted of killing his wife Carmela by lethal injection of succinylcholine. He was also acquitted of killing his lover's husband in the same manner. There are many people in the forensics field that, to this day, question whether he should have been convicted of his wife's murder. They say the testimony of the prosecution's so-called toxicology experts was flawed. Most experts today agree that he probably did kill her but that the evidence against him was not strong enough to support a finding of guilty beyond a reasonable doubt." There was a pause as he eyed the syringes. "Do you now what happens when succinylcholine is injected into your body?"

Again, Lizzy replied in the negative. Her mind was on one thing and one thing only–cutting herself free.

"It's a muscle relaxant. When anesthesiologists use it, they give the patient artificial respiration, but without that artificial respiration, the drug repeatedly stimulates and finally paralyzes respiratory muscles, causing respiratory failure and death." He squirted a small amount of liquid out of the needle. "There, all done. I think we're ready for our guest now."

Charley stood in the gravel parking lot, in the red glow of the neon vacancy sign, rubbing his chilled bones. Ten minutes passed before a motel room door opened. A shadow from the doorway called his name.

As he approached, he had no idea what he was walking into. About ten feet from the door, the makings of a face began to appear, but even as he got closer, the face was unrecognizable to him.

"Welcome, Charley," Grandstroke said, studying Charley's eyes. "You still don't recognize me?"

Charley shook his head. "Should I?"

"Just a little test," Grandstroke chortled as he stood at the doorway with arms crossed. Almost two months he'd kept Charley locked up after the accident, which, only he knew, was no accident at all. On a purely scientific level, he wondered how much, if anything, Charley would remember.

"Are you Grandstroke?"

Grandstroke's brows shot up. "What makes you say that?"

"I've read about you."

"What do you mean by that?"

"Dani's manuscript. You're the doctor she wrote of."

Grandstroke shook his head in disbelief. "You mean to tell me you *have* the manuscript? I can't believe it. I'd given up. I'd actually begun to doubt its very existence."

"So you knew about it?"

"Of course, I knew about it. Why do you think I killed her?"

Charley's ears pricked up. "Dani?"

"Of course." Grandstroke's chest swelled.

"What do you mean ... she ... I--" Charley stammered as he tried to sort it all out. "I saw her ... she grabbed the wheel."

"That's what I trained your mind to believe, Charley. The mind is a powerful tool, but it can be easily fooled. You had no memory of that accident until I tinkered with your brain."

"What did you do?"

"Simple thought reform."

"You mean brainwashing?"

Grandstroke conceded with a shrug. "Sure you can call it that. The fact is you had no memory. I gave you one. You should be thankful."

"So if she didn't die as I remember, how did she die?"

"I ran your car off the road with my own car. You were both unconscious but very much alive when I went back for you. I finished off your wife with a simple injection of a drug that I knew the medical examiner's autopsy would never detect, because I knew they wouldn't be looking for it. They just assumed she died from injuries from the crash."

Charley's face flushed with rage. "You fucking bastard. You killed all those girls. They weren't suicides at all. Dani was right. You're a fucking madman."

Altering his voice to a near-perfect impersonation of Jimmie Dart, Grandstroke said, "You barely know me at all. How dare you to judge me, you selfish little prick." He laughed uproariously.

Charley recognized the laugh. He'd heard it once before. "That was you," he sneered, now realizing that it had been Grandstroke, not Jimmie, who'd been the recipient of his punch that night at The Manhole.

Grandstroke smirked. "That was a pretty good punch you threw," he said, rubbing his jaw for effect.

"You killed him."

"The dirty business in the john. Yes, that was my handiwork. I particularly liked the extra touch of hanging him up by the skin on the coat hook. He looked so peaceful hanging there."

"You're mad."

"Stop playing doctor, Charley. I'm the only one licensed to make a diagnosis here." Grandstroke turned away and walked toward the bed, leaving the door ajar and Charley outside. After picking up the syringe he'd left on the bedside table, he sat down on the bed next to Lizzy and called out to Charley, "Are you going to stand out in the cold all night?"

Charley stepped into the dark, dingy motel room, lit only by a nightlight that shone over the bed. The doctor sat on the edge of the bed, wielding a hypodermic needle in his right hand and maintaining a tight hold on Lizzy. Fear showed in her eyes.

"Lizzy!" Charley cried. "Oh, my God! What have you done to her, you bastard?"

Grandstroke smiled mischievously. "So it comes down to this, a nice cozy threesome. Charley, I want you to pick up the needle and syringe that I've prepared for you, over there, on the dresser."

Charley did as instructed and then turned back to Grandstroke. "What do you want from me? I'll do anything you want. Just let her go."

"You know, Charley, I gave you a big clue early on that should have told you something was amiss."

"What the hell are you talking about?"

"The name ... Harold Yarac. Didn't Jimmie tell you he met me?"

"That was you?"

"Of course. I'm surprised you didn't pick up on the name. Yarac spelled backwards is Caray."

Charley shook his head as he gnawed on the inside of his mouth, disappointed that he hadn't seen it himself. "Harold Caray. Harry Caray."

"Clever, don't you think?" Grandstroke grinned with self-satisfaction. "You are the big Cubs fan. I thought for sure you'd figure it out. Harry Caray liked to turn ballplayer's names backwards. So I just turned his around and came up with my alter ego, Harold Yarac. I must say I was somewhat disappointed that you didn't catch that. It's no fun playing a one-sided game."

"Why all this game-playing? Why didn't you just kill me?"

"Don't you like to play games, Charley? I do."

"That doesn't explain anything," Charley said, bile rising in his stomach. "Why set me up as the killer?"

"I suppose partly it was just intellectual curiosity. I wanted to see what you'd do. You *do* interest me, Charley. More than that, I wanted that manuscript. The one you say you have. Since you've read it, you can see why I wouldn't want it ever to see the light of day. By framing you for murder, I was ensuring that would never happen."

When Lizzy's hands broke free, her eyes went wide, full of fear and excitement.

"Here's the deal," Grandstroke proclaimed. "Your girlfriend here lives, but only if you inject yourself with that hypodermic in your hand. You will die but it will be a relatively painless death and you will at least have the comfort of knowing that you saved at least one of your loves."

Charley shot a cautious eye. "Why should I trust you? Why should I believe you won't kill her?"

Grandstroke fired back a brash grin. Like any successful murderer, lying came naturally to him. "You shouldn't trust me, but, quite frankly, what choice do you have? I can kill her right now if I want to. This syringe that I'm holding is filled with the same poison that is in the syringe you're holding. But my promise to you is that I won't use it on her if you cooperate. I brought another vial, which contains a serum that I plan to use on your girlfriend here to make sure that she forgets everything about me. I will inject that into her and the only side effect will be some short-term memory loss. She will otherwise be able to lead a happy, normal life. So that's my proposition. Do we have a deal, Charley?"

Charley nodded, knowing he had no real option, and went about setting the hypodermic on the dresser, removing his jacket and lifting his left shirtsleeve. After he reached down and picked up the hypodermic, he closed his eyes and put the needle against his skin. Just as he was about to puncture the skin, he opened his eyes and glanced at Lizzy.

Her eyes found Charley's and she shook her head, sending him a signal he wasn't able to read ... until moments later when her arms shot out from behind her back. With all the strength she could muster, she wrestled Grandstroke's arms behind his back, causing him to drop the hypodermic.

"Stick him!" Lizzy cried.

From eight feet away, Charley launched his body, the hypodermic gripped in his upheld right hand. He landed like a linebacker on Grandstroke's chest, and in a swift, forceful motion, thrust the needle into his right arm.

Grandstroke wailed in pain, a broken rib having punctured his left kidney. Blood spurted from where the hypodermic remained lodged in his arm.

Charley maneuvered himself up and, for a moment, stood like a prizefighter over his beaten victim, and then he reached down and shoved him aside so that he could get to Lizzy. In a matter of seconds, he untied the knot that had held her ankles together, and then he grabbed her right hand and pulled her up.

They shot out the door, hand-in-hand, moving as one in a burst of adrenaline. They were free, they were together, and it felt good. That feeling, however, lasted only twenty feet. Charley had put the brakes on. "I've got to go back."

"Why?" Worry was etched on Lizzy's face.

"I don't have time to explain right now. Just keep running. I'll catch up to you."

"No. Don't go back. Just keep running."

Charley cupped his hands on Lizzy's shoulders and looked her in the eyes, asking her to believe in him one last time. "Trust me, Lizzy. I've got to do this." There would be time to explain later. He put her lips to his, the only way he could let her know that it would all work out and that he'd come back. When their lips met, he had to fight with himself to break them apart. There was one last piece of business to take care of, and it couldn't wait.

When he made it back to the motel room, Grandstroke lie flat on the floor like a dead piece of meat. The vultures would get their chance at him soon. Charley quivered at the sight of him. So much pain he had caused, but now it was all over. The bogeyman was dead.

Charley had come back for one thing–his jacket, which hung from the back of a chair. When he had it back in his hands, he made a run for it, not even taking a passing glance at the beaten body on the floor.

A couple of minutes later, Charley caught up with Lizzy. She was still running, down the dark road that had brought them there. From behind, he corralled her, wrapping his arms around her petite frame. At first, she was startled, but that was erased as soon as she glimpsed his face. A sense of relief overcame her. He'd come back, just as he'd promised. She peered into his eyes and smiled, and then she took his left hand and wrapped it in her right. "I'm not going to let go this time," she said.

"It's okay. He's dead. The past is behind us now."

About a half-mile down the road they came to the sleepy town of Thornton. When Lizzy pointed to a house with its lights on, they went to the door. Their knocking on the door went unanswered. When they cried for help, the lights inside of the house went dark.

As they stood at the door uncertain of what to do next, Charley saw the headlights of a car coming down the road and squeezed Lizzy's hand. They raced to flag it down, but the car sped by without slowing down.

Hand-in-hand they walked further down the road, content just to be together. About a minute later, they noticed the beam of a car's headlights creeping up from behind them. They turned and waved their arms. As the car approached they realized it wasn't slowing and at the last second Charley saw the face of the driver and pulled Lizzy away just before it sped by.

"What kind of maniacs do they have in this town?" Lizzy asked from her seat on the pavement.

"It was *him.*"

Lizzy's eyes widened.

Down the road, there was a squeal of brakes and a roar of an engine. Grandstroke was coming back for the kill.

"Run!" Charley cried. This was a fight between him and Grandstroke only.

Lizzy shook her head as she grabbed Charley's hand. "I told you before.

I'm not letting you go again." Tears streamed from her eyes.

There was no time to argue. Charley lifted himself, pulling Lizzy with him. Together they ran.

Their feet were no match for the eight cylinders of the Cadillac sedan that was bearing down on them. Together they dove for the gravel at the side of the road, but not in time for Charley's left hip to avoid getting swiped by the steel grill of the sedan. The smell of thick exhaust and the powder of the gravel choked them as they lie on the roadside. Charley grimaced as a sharp pain shot from his left hip and down the leg.

"Are you okay?" Worry stained Lizzy's face.

"Yeah, I think so." Truth was, his left leg was growing numb. He wasn't sure he'd be able to get up. "Can you help me up?"

Lizzy grabbed his hand and yanked him up. Down the road, tires squealed. He was coming for them–again.

Charley tried to run but was hobbled by the pain now shooting electrical shocks down his leg. "You go. Get help. I'll be okay."

Tears spilt from Lizzy's eyes. "No!" she cried. As she turned her head, the engine of the sedan roared again. The beam of the headlights blinded them.

"Run, Charley. You've got to run." She grabbed his hand and dragged him up. Wrapping an arm around her neck, she became his crutch. "Come on, Charley!"

Lizzy willed Charley along, but she could hear the roar of the engine closing in on them. She turned her head. The glow of the headlights was now touching them.

"Dive, Charley!"

Just as they dove to the roadside, dodging another hit, the drug that had been injected into Grandstroke took effect. At the wheel of the car, he convulsed violently and fell unconscious on the horn, which blared as the car flew down the road, whipping by the Village Hall, the fire station and Tully's Tavern. The sedan crashed through the gate protecting the limestone quarry at a speed of ninety miles per hour and nose-dived into the gaping hole, soaring in a graceful flight downward like a pelican swooping in on a school of minnows. Three hundred feet it fell until it met with limestone and exploded in a ball of fire.

Explosions from the quarry were not unusual. Limestone blasting went on there daily, shaking homes for miles around. So the explosion from the car didn't cause so much as a stir in the town, population two thousand five hundred eighty-two.

But Lester Figpole, who lived in Thornton for all of his seventy-eight years, and who worked down in the quarry for forty of those years, until he retired in 1975 and took a volunteer job as president of the local historical society, had a low tolerance for noisy kids, so he made a call to the home of his good friend, Tom Stonewall, the part-time police chief, to report what he thought had been a juvenile prank.

"I hope this is important, Lester. I'm right in the middle of 'Murder She Wrote.'" Lester was notorious for calling in what almost always turned out to be false alarms.

"There's some funny business goin' on outside, Tom. First, a couple of pranksters come knockin' on my door and start screamin' like wild hyenas, then some hot-rodder was racin' up and down the street. I think its those damn Huggins boys again."

"All right, Lester," the chief sighed, "I'll check on it."

Chief Stonewall parked his black-and-white squad car in front of Lester's house and got out to check things out. If there had been any kids messing around, it looked like they must have moved on. All was quiet now. Yet he sensed something had happened.

The air smelled of burnt rubber, so he pulled out his flashlight and shined it on the road. He noticed some fresh tire marks, which he followed for a block and a half until he was startled by the sight of Charley and Lizzy sitting on a curb. When he shined the flashlight on them, he saw that their clothes were torn and their faces were dusty, bruised and battered. "You folks need some help?"

Charley looked to Lizzy and then to the officer. "I'm Charley Hubbs."

Stonewall shined the flashlight in Charley's eyes. "I got a call about a disturbance out here. You folks know anything about that?"

"Officer, I'm telling you, I'm Charley Hubbs."

"Yeah, I heard you the first time. Is that supposed to mean something to me?"

Charley turned back to Lizzy, this time lifting his shoulders and turning his palms skyward. They both chuckled. Every cop in Chicago was looking for him but here he was in some sleepy little town, just twenty miles outside the city limits, and he was anonymous.

Charley turned his eyes back to the officer. "I'm turning myself in. I think you'll find somewhere in your records that I'm a wanted man in Chicago. In fact, if you have a copy of the *Chicago Herald* or the *Sun*, you'll probably see a not very flattering mug shot of me on the cover."

"Hey, wait a second now ... Hubbs ... you're that guy who's been on the lam for the last couple of days."

"That's me."

"Well, then, I've got to place you under arrest."

"That's right, officer." Charley struggled to get up. A swollen, painful, purplish bruise the size of a cantaloupe marked the area where his left hip had been sideswiped by the Cadillac sedan. He offered his wrists.

As he slapped the cuffs on Charley's wrists, Stonewall studied his catch. "So, I just got to ask, how in the hell did you end up here in my town, and why are you turning yourself in to me after running away from all the law enforcement in Chicago?"

"That's a long story. I think we'll have to sort that all out at the police station."

As the officer escorted Charley to the squad car, Charley mentioned to him that he'd find a hole in the chain-link fence surrounding the quarry just down the road and at the bottom of the quarry he'd find scattered pieces of a Cadillac sedan.

The officer directed Charley into the back seat of the squad car. Once Charley was in, he turned his attention to Lizzy. He advised her that a second squad would be by soon to pick her up. There'd be some questions for her back at the station.

Lizzy nodded. "Can I talk to him for a second?"

Stonewall didn't know what to think of what had happened in his town that night. This was the biggest catch he'd ever reeled in, and he hadn't even cast his line. The fish had come to him, jumping from the water, right into his bucket. "Yeah, go ahead," he shrugged.

Lizzy bent down and took in Charley, mist in her eyes. "Are you going to be okay?" She knew at that point no matter what the future held in store for them, she'd always be worried for him.

"I'll be fine," he assured. "How 'bout you?" He felt the same way she did. There would never be a day she would not be on his mind. They were brought together for a reason. He needed healing, and she needed someone to heal.

"I'm going to be okay." Tears now spilt from her eyes. "I'm just worried about you."

"Don't be. I'll be okay." He meant it, too.

"But how can you possibly prove your innocence now that he's dead?"

"Well, I've got you to testify on my behalf," he said with a warm smile, "and I've got this tape recorder in the inside pocket of my jacket."

Lizzy's eyes widened. "You taped all of that back in the motel room?"

"Yeah, maybe I'm not such a bad reporter after all."

The second squad pulled up and the police chief tapped Lizzy on the shoulder, indicating it was time for them to go. Lizzy nodded and stepped backwards away from the squad. While the second officer escorted her to the other squad, she kept her head turned and her eyes on Charley. After she was seated in the back seat, she turned her head again and smiled at Charley through the window. Then she pressed the palm of her right hand against the window, like she was touching his soul, telling him that all would be okay and, though they were separated now, they'd be together again. Of that she was now certain.

At the Thornton Police Station, Charley was taken into what had been described to him as the interrogation room. The chief apologized for the mess inside and hurriedly wiped off the food crumbs from the table and picked up two empty doughnut boxes.

"You can see we don't have many interrogations here."

When he finished tidying up, the chief asked to be excused, explaining that he needed to make some phone calls. A few minutes later, he returned and informed Charley that detectives from Chicago would be coming down to talk with him but that it would probably be about an hour before they arrived.

"Can I get you a cup of coffee?" There were many questions Stonewall had for Charley but they weren't his questions to ask. This was Chicago's business now.

"No, thank you … I was wondering if I could make one phone call, though."

"Oh, of course. How could I have forgotten?" The chief pointed Charley to a phone attached to the wall of the interrogation room and told him he'd leave him alone.

After he'd been given the job at the *Beat*, Buzz had handed Charley a business card with his home phone number on it. "This is only to be used for emergencies," Buzz had cautioned. If ever there was an emergency, this was it.

Charley glanced at the clock on the wall. It read 10:30 p.m. Tomorrow's front-page news had probably already gone to the printer.

Buzz was in bed reading *Men are from Mars, Woman are from Venus*, while his wife of 27 years, Lucy, slept next to him. When he heard Charley's voice, he had to check to make sure he wasn't dreaming. "You're supposed to be dead."

"I know, but I promise you, I'm very much alive. I called to tell you to do whatever you can in your power to make sure that tomorrow's paper doesn't get out on the streets with the story Piper wrote."

"I don't understand. How do *you* know what *Piper* wrote?"

Charley bit his lip. "Listen, I really don't have much time here. I'm just asking you to trust me and to do whatever you can in your power to make sure that story doesn't see the light of day."

"I'm really confused here. I got a call just an hour ago from Piper tellin' me he's got the story of the year– maybe of the century. He claimed you'd killed yourself and he had the exclusive story. So how can it be that you're still alive, and, if you're still alive, how the heck did Piper come up with this cockamamie story?"

"Tomorrow I'll explain it all to you. I'll give you a story like you've never seen. Just, whatever you do, make sure you stop that story."

Charley ended up receiving his first criminal conviction–not for the murders, but for his courthouse escape. Judge Foxtower lobbied hard for a sentence of at least thirty days, "If only to make a statement that such behavior would not be condoned in the courthouse." Donald "Pops" Donaldson, the courthouse's chief judge, saw that the only statement

Foxtower was trying to make was that he didn't want to come out looking like the fool he obviously was. In Judge Donaldson's estimation, Charley had already been put through the wringer, so he slapped him with one year of probation and thirty days of community service. Donaldson silenced Foxtower by transferring him to traffic court.

As he'd promised Buzz, Charley wrote his own exclusive story, a vivid first-hand account of his escape from the clutches of a mass-murderer. The paper sold out throughout the city for weeks afterward and the story garnered the *Beat* national coverage. Charley was interviewed on *Good Morning America*, *The Today Show*, even *Nightline*. Each time he appeared humble, expressed his gratitude for the support of his newspaper, and gave special mention to Lizzy. "She deserves all the credit in the world," he said in interview after interview. "Without her, I don't think I'd be alive today."

Alive. When he used that word, he meant it not only in the physical sense. There was an emotional level as well. In many ways, he'd died when Dani had died. Lizzy, however, had breathed new life into him.

The truth about Piper Charley kept from Buzz. He knew it would only hurt him. There were many things Charley never did tell Buzz. This was for the best. Sometimes the truth was just too painful.

Two days after Charley's story hit the newsstands, Piper was found in his apartment, slumping in a blood stained La-Z-Boy, a fist-sized hole in the back of his skull. A high-velocity .38-caliber bullet was found lodged in the wall behind the chair. A black barrel Smith and Wesson revolver was on the floor.

"I can't believe this," Buzz said, hovering over Charley with a big, hairy paw resting on his shoulder. "Can you?" After working up a solemn face, Charley turned and shook his head. "I mean to kill yourself because you screwed up on a story. I just can't believe it … and he was such a good reporter before that. Almost twenty-five years… I just can't understand what happened. I try and try, but it makes no sense to me. I mean he didn't even leave a suicide note. I know he was drinkin' a lot … you think that's what did it?"

Charley returned a sobering eye. "Hard to say what makes people do the things they do."

Epilogue
When the going gets Tuffy

Opening Day, April 4, 1994

The stringy vines, barren and brown from the long winter, clung to the red brick of the outfield wall as if they were grasping for life from the old ballpark. Wrigley Field had come out of hibernation after six months of winter, holding in it the hope of spring. By June, the vines would be in full blossom, painting the wall a brilliant green.

Opening day of the baseball season meant a new beginning. On opening day anything was possible. You could put the previous years behind you and start from scratch. On opening day it didn't matter that the Cubs had not won a World Series in eighty-six years. They were on equal footing with every other team.

For Charley, it meant a new beginning, too. Sitting in the centerfield bleachers, ten rows back from the wall, he glanced at Lizzy, sitting to his right, and smiled. Being there with her felt right. Now he could put his past behind him and move on.

For Lizzy, too, it meant a fresh start. She also had a past she was ready to put behind her. Although she didn't know what the future held for them, she was willing to take a chance. So often before she put up her guard and pushed them away. This time she vowed not to make the same mistake.

Lizzy breathed it all in, the smell of hot dogs and beer, the buzz of the crowd, the beauty of the old ballpark. For her, it was a nostalgic trip back to childhood, to when she was eight years old, sitting in the left field bleachers, starry-eyed, with her father.

"You're daydreaming," Charley said.

Lizzy smiled. "I'm sorry. I was just thinking."

"About what?"

"How amazing it feels to be here."

"With me?" Charley teased. By now, Charley knew what she was thinking. Her thoughts at that moment had nothing to do with him, and that was okay.

"Yeah," she said with a flirtatious push and a bat of the lashes.

"You think the two of us have a chance?"

They'd been living together, in Lizzy's apartment, for a month now. Charley had abandoned his studio, which held too many haunting memories and not enough furniture for the two of them. Things were good between them. He kept telling her he wanted to marry her but she kept telling him to give it time.

"Sure we've got a chance." She put her hands together between her legs, leaned back and closed her eyes. "I can't believe I've been away from this place so long."

When she opened her eyes, she was startled to see a baseball coming right at her. Acting on instinct, she stood on her bleacher seat and put her arms up in the air. The ball fell in the palms of her hands as she fell back into the crowd behind her.

Charley's jaw dropped in amazement. "Oh, my God!" He reached for her and pulled her back up.

Lizzy grinned and shrugged her shoulders. "I guess this is my lucky day. Who hit it?"

Charley turned and saw the name on the scoreboard. "You just caught a home run ball off the bat of Tuffy Rhodes."

Lizzy studied the ball, holding it as if it had magical powers. "Tuffy Rhodes … I like that name. Do you think this is a sign?"

"A sign? What do you mean?"

"Of good things to come."

Charley looked at her curiously. There was a playful, childlike quality in her he hadn't witnessed before. She was that wide-eyed eight-year-old, filled with awe and wonderment.

"We all follow roads, Charley. Ours just happens to be named Tuffy." As she raised her head and turned toward Charley, a slow grin surfaced.

Charley nudged her and smiled as he shook his head. "You scared me for a second there. I thought just maybe you were getting in touch with your inner-Cub, that you might actually be an optimist."

Lizzy laughed heartily. For the first time in a long time, she was having fun. "I'll tell you what, if Tuffy hits another out here, I'll believe anything can happen."

Charley returned a skeptical eye. "Even the Cubs winning a World Series?"

"Some things are beyond the realm of belief," she deadpanned. "But then again…"

Postscript

Karl "Tuffy" Rhodes was a little known prospect who'd played in less than a hundred games in the major leagues before the Cubs gave him the nod on April 4, 1994, opening day of the season. He raised the hopes of all Cubs fans that day, when he became the first National League player to hit three home runs on opening day. Despite Rhodes' heroics, the Mets beat the Cubs twelve to eight, with Dwight "Doc" Gooden getting the win over Mike Morgan.

The Cubs' loss that day was a sign of things to come. A record home losing streak of twelve games was finally snapped on May 4, with help from a *good luck* goat in attendance. (In Cubs lore, the team's misfortunes can be traced to an eternal hex placed on them by William "Billy" Sianis, owner of a saloon called Billy Goat's. Sianis brought his favorite goat to a game at Wrigley Field during the 1945 World Series, but ushers escorted Sianis and his goat out of the ballpark. In retaliation, Sianis put what became known as the Billy Goat Hex on the team. The Cubs lost that series to Detroit in seven games and have not returned to the World Series since then.)

The Cubs would go on to finish the strike-shortened 1994 season in last place with a 49-64 record.

Rhodes' career in the major leagues went down the drain after that game as well. He managed just five more homers the rest of the season and finished a five-year major league career in 1995 with a total of thirteen home runs and a .225 batting average.

That was not by any means the end of Rhodes' baseball career, though. In 1996, he signed with the Osaka Kinetsu Buffaloes in Japan, where he quickly became a fan favorite. During the 2001 season, Rhodes tied the Japan pro baseball single-season home run record of fifty-five, formerly achieved by Sadaharu Oh of the Yokiuri Giants.

The Cubs, meanwhile, still wait for glory to shine on them again. The last time was 1908.

Yet in the eyes of all Cubs fans, there's always next year and the hope of spring is eternal. Next year could be this year.